PATTI JO MOORE

A Seaside Romance

Patti Jo Moore

Published by Forget Me Not Romances, a division of Winged Publications

Copyright © 2017 by Patti Jo Moore

All rights reserved. No part of this publication may be resold, reproduced, stored in a retrieval system, or transmitted in any form or by any means, electronic, mechanical, recording, or otherwise, without the prior written permission of the author. Piracy is illegal. Thank you for respecting the hard work of this author.

This is a work of fiction. All characters, names, dialogue, incidents, and places either are the product of the author's imagination or are used fictitiously. Any resemblance to actual events, locales, or people, living or dead, is entirely coincidental.

ISBN-13: 979-8-8690-7319-8

Dedicated to all my family and friends who have encouraged me in my writing journey. With very special thanks to Hugh Moore, Dr. Amy Moore, Becca Manny, Steven Moore, Shaun Manny, John Hugens, Janet Harris, and Nancy Stryker. Also thanks to Kathy Scogin, Vickie Starkey, Norma Clements, Susan Crutchfield, Pam Guimarin, Celia Ledbetter, Terry Matthews, Tracie Robbins, Shannon Davis, and Dr. Bernie Toole. A special shout-out to Cynthia Hickey, Sherri Stewart, Tina Radcliffe, and my Writing Sisters. Most of all, thank you to my Lord and Savior Jesus Christ, who loves me and blesses me abundantly.

1

Emma Jean Hopkins gazed out the window of her bungalow, enjoying a dolphin close to the shore. Past the beach of sugary sand, she watched the creature leap playfully in the teal water, the sun shimmering on its slick skin. *Not a care in the world.* Would she ever feel that way again?

After all, wasn't the reason she moved to Coastal Breeze, Florida, to forget about her past and move forward, without having to look over her shoulder all the time? Her ringing cell phone snapped her from her thoughts.

A smile spread across her face as Jeb Hopkins' southern drawl came through the phone. "How's my favorite daughter doing today?" He chuckled in his customary good-natured way, and Emma could visualize her overall-clad father standing by the kitchen window of the cozy farm home, sipping his morning coffee.

She giggled. "Hi, Dad. Your favorite—and

only—daughter is doing fine, thanks. How are you? I hope the farm isn't making you work too hard." Concern laced her voice for her sixty-two-year old father exerting himself on the twenty-acre family farm in South Georgia.

"Nah, don't worry none about me. Working hard is what keeps me going, you know. Besides, these farmhands I got are a big help." He cackled, and Emma could envision his tanned face and whiskered chin.

Without warning a twinge of something—homesickness?—tugged at her heart, and she drew in a deep breath. If her father thought for one second she was homesick, he'd hop in his pick-up truck and drive to the Florida panhandle as fast as he could.

Besides, he had been through enough in the past two years with problems on the farm and the loss of Emma's mother, so he wouldn't want his baby girl to be unhappy.

She continued talking so he wouldn't suspect a hint of melancholy had crept in. "I think that once I adjust to my new town and get into a routine of running the gift shop, everything will be great. I can't wait for you to come and visit." She prepared herself for her father's usual response whenever he was invited anywhere.

"I'd love to see you, Em. But you know how busy this farm keeps me. And I sure don't have the energy I used to, especially with my ol' arthritis acting up now and then. I promise you I'll get down there one of these days, and you know you can call me anytime if you need anything."

"I know, Dad. Thanks. And don't worry—Aunt Ginny has been wonderful." Fighting the lump in her throat, she changed the subject by inquiring about her favorite goat and the other farm animals. Ten minutes later their call ended.

Okay, time to get going. She finished the last few swigs of her coffee and got dressed. Tomorrow the gift shop would be reopening, but today she'd dress in jeans and a tee shirt, with minimum makeup. No sense in wearing better clothes if she was going to be by herself most of the day arranging items on shelves, checking inventory lists, and general cleaning duties.

Heading out of the cottage, Emma breathed in the warm April air blowing in from the gulf. She pulled her chestnut hair into a ponytail and lifted her face to the sunshine. Sometimes she still couldn't believe she lived at the Florida coast. The view of the ocean from her windows often made her feel she was dreaming, especially when the dolphins were frolicking along the emerald coast.

Before climbing into her car for the short drive to her aunt's shop, Emma noticed the brilliant blue sky. Puffs of clouds floated toward the west, reminding her of cotton balls her mother had always kept in a small jar in their home.

Mother. How she missed her sweet mom, though Emma would not have wanted the poor woman to linger in pain any longer. The horrible cancer had ravaged Shirley Hopkins' body and her passing had been a blessing in that respect. Yet grief had overwhelmed Emma and her family at the time, and two years hadn't lessened her sense of loss.

After parking in the small lot adjacent to the store, Emma hurried to the glass door and knocked. She grinned as she saw her aunt hurrying to let her in.

"Good morning, my sweet niece." Aunt Ginny planted a quick kiss on Emma's cheek, then drew back and looked at her. "Even dressed casually for work, you're still a beauty, Emma Jean. It amazes me that you're not married with a couple of little ones around you." The middle-aged woman clicked her tongue before continuing. "But when the right man does come along, you'll be ready. I still hate what you went through with that no-good thug, may he rest in peace." Ginny shook her head, then grabbed Emma's hand and pulled her to the counter.

"I'm just happy you've offered me this opportunity to live and work in Coastal Breeze, Aunt Ginny. It's so different from being on the farm, but I already like it a lot."

"Well, I'm sure the scenery is different, but I guess the heat and humidity are what you're used to." Her aunt smiled.

"Oh yes, good ol' South Georgia summers are plenty hot and humid, but at least here there's a nice breeze from the ocean." She released a sigh and smiled. "I really do think I'll be happy here." Eager to get to work, Emma was certain her social-butterfly aunt had things to do.

"I sure hope and pray you are, sweetheart. Now, you've got my cell number if you need me today. I'm meeting my stitchery group for lunch over in Destin, and then plan to run a few errands. But I can scoot back here in a flash if you need me.

Remember to keep the door locked and I've got snacks and soft drinks in the supply room, so help yourself."

After a few general instructions about a small amount of inventory to be listed and shelved, Ginny was out the door, her citrusy cologne scenting the air behind her.

To Emma's relief the time passed quickly, and she didn't have any problems with the jobs she needed to accomplish. Who knows? Maybe running a small gift shop would be a good fit for her and she'd enjoy it much more than she'd expected. It would certainly be different than working in the daycare center back in her hometown.

About one o'clock, her stomach rumbled, and she decided she needed more than snack crackers and a bottled water. After locking the gift shop, she drove to a nearby fast-food restaurant and picked up her lunch.

The cheeseburger, fries, and cola weren't the healthiest choice for a midday meal, but today it would do and it gave her a boost of energy. About an hour after eating, Emma was rearranging some figurines on a shelf when a knock sounded at the door.

The noise startled her so much she almost dropped a small mouse figurine. Her heart pounded as she tried to decide whether to answer the door or duck down and hide behind a shelf. *Oh, good grief, don't be ridiculous. The person has most likely seen you already, and maybe whoever it is only needs directions.* Not that she'd be much help in that area.

Slowly making her way toward the glass door,

Emma was surprised to see a well-dressed man who appeared to be close to her age. With neatly trimmed brown hair and dark eyes, he was tall, and his business suit seemed to emphasize his broad shoulders. Was Aunt Ginny expecting a sales representative today? No, her organized aunt would've mentioned that, and she would not have left Emma on her own.

With shaking hands, she inched the door open and gazed up at the stranger. "Yes?" To her dismay the one word came out as a timid squeak, much like the mouse figurine she'd almost dropped might make had it been a real mouse.

The man smiled with a curious tilt of his head. "I'm sorry, is this store not open?"

Aaaugh…she'd forgotten to hang the CLOSED sign on the door. Emma reached up and tucked some wayward strands of hair behind her ear as she attempted to maintain a calm and confident manner, even though she was nowhere close to feeling that way at the moment.

"No, I'm sorry but the gift shop is closed until tomorrow. We'll be opening at ten o'clock in the morning." For some strange reason she had the sudden urge to invite the stranger inside the store and offer him one of the colas that Aunt Ginny kept in the supply room. No! She didn't know this man and absolutely could not permit him to step inside the shop.

She was relieved when he nodded and gave her a wide grin—one that only made his handsome face even more handsome.

"Okay, no problem. Sorry I disturbed you."

"Oh, you didn't disturb me. I was just doing some work since the shop reopens tomorrow. I'd forgotten to hang the CLOSED sign on the door, and I'm really sorry we're not open yet." What was wrong with her? She was rambling like a lonely person starved for attention.

"Well, since you'll be open tomorrow, I'll try to stop by on my way back home to Alabama." He hesitated as if wanting to say more, but didn't. "Thank you again." With a pleasant nod, the good-looking stranger turned and headed toward his sleek sports car parked in the adjacent lot.

She stood at the door and stared as he walked away, and for a reason she couldn't explain, she had a letdown feeling as he climbed into his car. *Get a grip, Emma.* For all she knew this man could be some kind of con artist or have a sketchy background. It was probably a blessing he didn't linger any longer.

Yet returning to her task of arranging figurines, she found herself hoping he'd stop by the next day. Even if he didn't purchase anything, she wanted to see him again.

~ ~ ~

Why had he knocked on the gift shop door? It should've been obvious that the store wasn't open for business. Yet he'd been eager to purchase a birthday gift for his sister and he knew Avril would appreciate something from the Florida coast.

On second thought, maybe it had been a blessing he'd knocked at the door because the pretty worker who answered was a sight for his tired, overworked eyes. As if to emphasize how hard he had been working lately, his cell phone rang at that moment.

"Thomas Wilton here." He hoped his voice didn't carry the exhaustion he felt.

"Hello Thomas. It's Mac Chandler, in the main office. Am I catching you at a bad time?"

Thomas's pulse quickened, and his hand gripped the steering wheel tightly. Maybe he should pull off the road into a parking lot somewhere so he could focus on this conversation. It wasn't everyday he received a phone call from the company's co-founder.

"Hello, Mr. Chandler. No, this is fine. I'm just driving back to my hotel in Destin at the moment, so I can talk." Yeah, he definitely needed to pull off the road. Thankfully a fast-food restaurant was up ahead so he was able to whip into the small parking lot.

Breathing a sigh of relief, he could now focus on the call. He grabbed his satchel in the passenger seat with his free hand and took out a small notebook and a pen. It might not be a bad idea to jot notes as Mr. Chandler talked—especially given how tired he was at the moment.

"Well, I'm glad I caught you, because we've recently had a board meeting and you've been recommended to take over the Florida territory for Coastal Industries. I'd much prefer giving you this information in person, but I wanted to go ahead and let you know so you could give it some thought. Now, don't feel pressured about letting us know. Take some time to pray over this major decision and career move. You can take up to two weeks if needed, because the position will involve continued traveling and handling a bit more work. But we're always here to support you, so don't ever feel you're in this alone. You can call on myself or Ben Groves at any time with questions or if you need additional help. I do hope you'll consider this offer and give it serious thought. And by the way, it also includes a ten-percent pay increase, so that's something else to consider. Since you're a single man, you might not have a lot of expenses at the moment. However, once you settle down and have a family, this added income would be mighty handy." Mr. Chandler chuckled, his southern accent prominent in his comments.

Thomas knew it was a blessing he'd pulled off the main road and into a parking lot, otherwise he might've swerved onto the curb as he heard his boss's reason for calling.

A few seconds of silence hung in the air before Thomas cleared his throat and attempted to sound professional. "Thank you, Mr. Chandler. This is certainly an unexpected offer, and I'm deeply humbled and grateful. I will give this serious thought and let you know within the two-week time frame. You have my word." *Good grief, I sound like I'm negotiating a deal between two countries.* Yet at that moment he felt more honored and esteemed than he ever had, so for him this was a huge deal.

After a few more general comments about the weather and the current baseball season, the call ended. Thomas sat for a few minutes, absorbing the news he'd just received. He wasn't sure if he felt like giving a whoop of joy or shuddering at the giant workload he knew would be placed upon his shoulders should he accept this position. But one thing was certain, and that was how fortunate he was to work at a Christian-based company who valued their employees. Yes, he had a lot of praying to do.

The next morning Thomas hurried to his car, clutching a cup of hotel coffee. He'd already checked out and his one bag was in his trunk. Now he'd head to his appointment with a hotel manager in Miramar, and then he was free to drive back home to Alabama. Except for one stop in Coastal Breeze. Yes, he'd swing by the little gift shop and purchase something for his sister. At the thought of seeing the pretty woman he'd spoken with the day before, his heart rate quickened. What was wrong with him? He knew absolutely nothing about her except for the fact she worked in a gift shop in a tiny coastal community.

Focus on this meeting. He chided himself while pulling into the large hotel parking lot. Palm trees swayed in the warm morning breeze and a few hotel guests walked to and from their cars. It was only April, yet most of the hotels were already doing a heavy business. In the peak tourist season of summer, it would be packed, he knew.

Entering the well-furnished lobby, Thomas was thankful he'd worn a nice suit. This hotel was upscale compared to many of their other clients. A clerk behind the guest counter smiled, eyeing him with appreciation. Her blond hair and tanned skin seemed to echo the fact she worked at a coastal hotel and was no doubt in the sun a lot. With brightly-painted nails and matching lipstick, she would be considered attractive to many men, yet Thomas tended to shy away from that look. The image of his previous girlfriend flashed in his mind. He shoved away the bitter memories of his last relationship.

"May I help you?" The clerk leaned toward the counter and her strong perfume reached Thomas's nose, making it itch.

"Good morning. I have a ten o'clock appointment with Mr. Wallace."

The woman's eyes lingered on his face a moment, making him feel awkward. He was more than ready to have this meeting and move on with his day.

The clerk looked down at a ledger on the counter and nodded. "Yes, Mr. Wallace should be in the main meeting room. I'm sure it's been reserved for the two of you to meet privately. I'll take you to him." She stepped out from behind the counter and wiggled a finger at him, indicating he was to follow.

He was thankful Ms. Clerk with the heavy make-up and perfume wouldn't be in their meeting. Not usually one to judge, Thomas couldn't help being a little wary of this woman.

She walked slowly in her stiletto heels down a carpeted hallway, then stopped at a closed door. Tapping lightly, she leaned toward the door and called out Mr. Wallace's name.

Then she quickly turned back to Thomas and winked. "He's all yours. Have a nice meeting." She stiletto-walked her way back down the hall toward the lobby, leaving the heavy perfume scent trailing behind.

Just as Thomas stepped into the meeting room, he sneezed. *Great. What a way to enter a meeting with a client.* Reaching into his pocket, he lifted out a linen handkerchief—silently thanking his grandmother for the gift many Christmases ago—and tried to discreetly wipe his nose.

Mr. Wallace stood from the table and smiled, extending a hand. "Good morning, Thomas. I hope my directions were helpful and you didn't get lost in the maze of hotels." The large man laughed good-naturedly, putting Thomas at ease.

"No sir, your directions were perfect. Thank you for meeting with me today, Mr. Wallace."

"Please, call me Chip. No formalities here." With a shake of his head and a slight grin, he continued. "I see you've met Devonna, one of our clerks." He blew out a sigh that could be interpreted as frustration. "Please don't misunderstand me, since we've only just met. But she's the hotel owner's daughter and that is why she works at the main desk. That's all I'll say for now." The look he gave Thomas backed up his own first impressions of the woman. It would appear that Chip Wallace wasn't thrilled with the image Devonna presented to those entering the hotel.

"Would you like some coffee? Or cola or water? The temperature is already climbing today, I can feel it."

Thomas politely declined, then opened his business satchel and took out his notebook. He was pleased with Chip Wallace's reaction to the suggestions he outlined for the hotel.

To his delight, Thomas was out of the meeting in under two hours. And there was no further communication with the clerk. He strode briskly toward his car enjoying the bright sunshine streaming down on him and hearing the distant squawk of gulls, searching for their lunch at the nearby beach. He inhaled a deep breath of ocean air, feeling positive that this would be a good day. After all, with the exception of the staring clerk, everything else had gone great. Now to head to Coastal Breeze, then home to Alabama.

Driving along the main highway that led into Coastal Breeze, he pondered gift ideas for Avril. What would give his handicapped sister a big smile? She liked so many things, but he wanted to give her something really special.

About ten minutes later he pulled into the parking lot for *Ginny's Treasures by the Sea,* and noticed a few other cars in the lot, which was a good sign. Thomas always felt sorry for small, independent businesses that couldn't compete with large chain stores.

As he opened the door, a small bell tinkled overhead, and a delightful scent of something fresh and citrusy greeted him. Would he see the pretty employee he'd spoken with the previous day? Instead, an older woman greeted him and he felt a stab of disappointment.

"Welcome to Ginny's. May I help you find something today?" She wore a turquoise dress with bright jewelry and her voice was warm. Despite the fact she must be in her sixties, she exuded energy and had a youthful sparkle in her eyes.

"Thank you. I'm looking for a gift for a twenty-three-year-old woman. I guess I'll just look around, if that's okay."

"Oh certainly, honey. You take your time, but if you need help let me know. And by the way, my name is Ginny so feel free to holler if you need assistance." She gave him another warm smile before turning to help two women who were asking her opinion about a small lamp.

He thanked her and gathered his wits to see what was available in the shop. Specifically, he needed something that Avril would really like.

Scented candles were displayed in an attractive setting, with tiny seashells sprinkled among them. As Thomas moved on, he saw figurines—most with a nautical theme—and other small decorative items for someone's home—gift baskets, scented lotions, jewelry, small ocean-themed framed prints, and even greeting cards. He decided Ginny had an eclectic kind of gift shop, carrying an assortment of items. Now, what to buy for his sister?

A female voice spoke and he jerked his head to the right. The woman from the day before! Except today she looked even prettier.

She smiled at him. "Did you need some help?"

He tried not to stare. Was she the same woman? Yes, it had to be. Yet today she was dressed in nicer clothes—not fancy, but a coral-colored Capri outfit with a small sailboat stitched on the front. Her shoulder-length chestnut hair hung loosely, framing a pretty face with green eyes and a mouth that looked as if it smiled easily. For some reason the word *wholesome* came to mind. A far cry from the hotel clerk he'd encountered earlier that day. Or his ex-girlfriend, Courtney.

Thomas shrugged. "Thanks, I'm just looking around. I need a gift for a twenty-three-year-old woman, so I'm sure I'll find something here she'll like."

"Okay, I'm Emma if you need any help. And my Aunt Ginny is here too if you have questions. I'm new and still learning, but I'm happy to help any way I can." She offered another smile, then turned and headed to a customer trying to decide on some earrings.

Thomas remained where he was, watching Emma walk away. He'd glanced at her hands and hadn't noticed a ring, but that didn't always mean anything. Why did he feel so drawn to her?

Snapping himself out of his thoughts about the beautiful employee, he stepped over to the scented lotions and sniffed a couple of bottles. Yes, Avril would like these. One was honeysuckle and the other jasmine. Not too heavy, but nice feminine scents.

Clutching the two bottles of lotion, he was about to head to the counter to pay but stopped. His attention was captured by a small lighthouse figurine, and he knew Avril would love it. Carefully lifting it from the display, he then stepped to the checkout counter to pay.

No one was behind the counter, so he stood there with the items placed near the register.

"Are you ready?" Emma hurried toward him.

"Yes, these should be perfect." He grinned and

took out his wallet.

Emma rang up the lotions and the lighthouse, then wrapped everything before placing the items in a bag. As she reached her hand out to accept his payment, their hands touched.

Her skin was so smooth. Did she notice their contact? The quick glance she gave him answered his silent question.

A shy, hesitant smile slightly curved Emma's lips, and she ducked her head as she placed the money into the cash register drawer. "Thank you for shopping at Ginny's. If you're in the area again, please feel free to stop by."

Was she giving him a standard line she was trained to use on customers, or could she possibly want him to stop by again?

He gave a smiling nod. "Thank you, Emma. I'll definitely be in the area again since I travel for my job, so I'm sure I'll stop here in the future. Your aunt has a very nice shop."

She reached up and tucked a strand of hair behind one ear, revealing a small sailboat earring. "Yes, Aunt Ginny has worked hard and is very proud of her little shop. I've recently moved here to help her run it."

"Oh? Where are you from?"

"South Georgia. I grew up on a farm in the tiny town of Westville. You've probably never heard of it." She giggled, a blush tinting her pretty face.

Thomas feigned a frown and laughed. "No, sorry I haven't. I'm from the Montgomery area of Alabama, but travel in Florida for my job. I'm with Coastal Industries, and you've probably never heard of that company." He laughed again, pleased to see her grinning as she shook her head. Then he added. "My name is Thomas, by the way. Thomas Wilton."

She grinned, but then someone else caught her attention, and Thomas realized two women were standing behind him waiting to pay for their purchases. He needed to leave but didn't want to. As he said good-bye, he promised to stop in her aunt's shop again.

Driving back to Alabama, Thomas couldn't stop thinking about the attractive employee. She was a farm girl from South Georgia now working in a small gift shop on the Florida coast. What a different life this must be for her.

As he continued the three-hour drive, various thoughts whirled through his mind. The phone call from Mr. Chandler offering the promotion, his meeting with the hotel manager that morning, and meeting an attractive lady named Emma who worked in a gift shop. Yet the one thought that dominated and pleased him the most was thinking of Emma, and Thomas knew without a doubt he would be stopping by that shop again. The sooner the better.

~ ~ ~

Why had she babbled on so much to that customer? Sure, he was attractive and tall and wore a nice business suit. Not to mention his sleek little sports car. But for all Emma knew he might be married. Yeah, she'd heard stories of businessmen who traveled and met women in different cities and deceived them. No, she absolutely would not let herself be deceived again—ever. After what she'd experienced with BG she could never go through that again.

"Emma, you've worked so hard today, honey. It's almost two o'clock and you need to eat your lunch. Go on to the supply room and take a break. I can handle the shop, and I've already munched some snacks between my customers, so I'm not hungry." Ginny patted her shoulder and Emma knew it would do no good to argue with her aunt.

"Okay, I'll eat the sandwich I brought, but if it gets busy out here, you holler. I won't be long." She wasn't about to tell her aunt she doubted if she could even get down the peanut butter sandwich she'd brought. After her brief chat with Thomas, her stomach had been doing cartwheels.

Yet as she nibbled at her sandwich and small bag of chips, she remembered that Thomas had mentioned he was purchasing a gift for a twenty-three-year-old woman. Hmm…possibly his girlfriend? What did it matter? She might never see him again.

She didn't have time to mull over that last thought because the chattering she heard from the shop indicated business had picked up. Her aunt would need her help, so Emma took another sip of cola and hurried out to assist.

Ginny looked at her in amazement. Sure enough, there were now close to twenty customers milling around the shop. Hopefully these people weren't only browsing because more sales would help prepare for the upcoming summer season.

Pasting on a smile, Emma stepped over to an older lady who was admiring the jewelry selection.

"Did you need any help?"

"No thank you, dear. I'm just looking, but I have a feeling I'll be purchasing one of these bracelets. They are so cute with the little nautical charms on them."

"Yes, ma'am, they are. I confess those are one of my favorite items in Aunt Ginny's shop." She grinned at the elderly lady, who had on bright pink lipstick that matched a pink ensemble she wore, including dangling pink flamingo earrings.

The woman paused and eyed Emma. "Is Ginny your aunt? Is that what you said, dear? My hearing isn't so keen anymore." She chuckled and shook her head, the curls in her silver hair bouncing along with her earrings.

"Yes, ma'am. I'm Ginny's niece, Emma Hopkins. I've recently moved here from South Georgia to help out in the gift shop."

"That is wonderful! So nice to meet you, Emma. My name is Mildred Weatherbee, but my friends call me Midge. I know Ginny from church, and of course, the times when I've shopped here." She continued smiling at Emma, then reached out and lifted a bracelet from the small stand. "I think I will go ahead and buy this, and I'll be stopping in again soon. I need to get on to the grocery store before my legs give out. Ah, the joys of getting old." She chuckled and shook her head.

After ringing up the sale, Emma smiled at her. "It was nice to meet you, Mrs. Weatherbee." She handed the small bag across the counter.

The woman laughed and playfully shook a finger at her. "I insist you call me Midge. Besides, it'll make me feel younger." She laughed again as Emma agreed to use her nickname.

After the woman exited the shop, Ginny hurried over to Emma. "Oh, I didn't get to speak to Midge. She's a sweetheart, although some folks think she's a bit of a busybody. But she means well." Ginny straightened a few knick-knacks at the counter, then peered directly at her niece. "How are things going for you? Not too overwhelming, I hope. Please don't tell me you're ready to return to the farm." She winked and reached out to pat Emma's hand.

"No worries. It's going well, and I guess I shouldn't spend so much time on one customer, but that lady was very kind." Emma was relieved when her aunt assured her she was going a great job.

"Besides, if my customers don't feel they're getting a warm welcome and friendly service, they can easily shop elsewhere." She grinned before hurrying off to assist several women in the home décor section.

The remainder of the day passed quickly, even though business tapered off closer to suppertime. Emma was surprised at how tired she was and looked forward to the soft bed in her cottage.

"Are you sure you don't want to come to my house for supper? I've got a leftover casserole to reheat and it would be plenty to share." Ginny eyed her with a bit of concern.

"That's so sweet, but I'll be fine. I stocked my refrigerator and pantry with enough food to hold me awhile, and I'll heat up some soup and do some reading tonight. Thank you anyway." It gave Emma a sense of security knowing she wasn't all alone in her new town. Not that she had anyone to fear in Coastal Breeze—the dangers had been left behind in South Georgia.

A few minutes later she unlocked her cottage door, glad to be home. As she enjoyed her soup and relaxed that evening, her mind returned to her day at the gift shop. At least being so busy had prevented her from dwelling on the handsome customer earlier in the day. But she couldn't deny that she hoped he'd stop in her aunt's store again. Very soon.

PATTI JO MOORE

2

As Thomas watched his younger sister lift her gifts out of the bag, a lump formed in his throat. Even though Avril was fine mentally, the fact that her physical actions took longer and often required deliberate concentration and effort still got to him. As so often happened, flashes of her in previous years scurried through his mind. Avril as a little girl, running and playing like a normal kid. Then as an outgoing teenager, a pretty, popular cheerleader, proud of the cartwheels and splits she could do.

Shoving those bittersweet memories from his mind, Thomas forced himself to focus on the present and seeing his sister's face radiate true pleasure from the little gifts he'd brought her.

"Oh Thomas…this lotion smells so nice." She took a slow sniff after he'd opened the top for her, another painful reminder of her limitations. She took another sniff and awkwardly held the bottle out to him. "Want to wear some? I'll share." She giggled.

That was his little sister—still teasing him even as she sat in a wheelchair.

He chuckled, took a step back, and held up his hands. "No thanks. That is for you. I don't need to smell like a girl when I meet with clients." It warmed his heart to see her giggle and tease him.

"There's something besides lotion in the gift bag." He gestured to the pink bag he'd located in his mom's gift wrapping supplies after arriving home that day. He'd wanted the items to be presented in a way that made her feel special, and nothing like a fancy little pink bag to please his sister.

"What? You brought me two bottles of lotion. That's plenty, and you didn't have to do that." She gazed up at him with understanding in her eyes. Yes, she knew that he still carried a burden for her present condition. He could read it in her hazel eyes.

"It's just a little something, but I saw it and knew you'd like it. At least I hope you do. If not, next time Mom has a garage sale you can offer that." He grinned, knowing that would get a reaction from Avril.

Sure enough, she gasped. "No way I'm putting a special gift from my brother in a garage sale." She lifted out the tissue-wrapped lighthouse figurine. After painstakingly pulling off the tissue paper, her eyes welled with tears. "Oh Thomas, it's beautiful." She continued gazing at the figurine she held.

He swallowed the lump in his throat and knew he needed to say something silly to lighten the mood before he showed his emotional side. Not intending to verbalize his thoughts, the comment slipped out. "Yeah, the cashier at the gift shop was beautiful too."

Oh great. Why did I say that? Avril stared up at him with a mixture of amusement and shock as Thomas shook his head. "But that's not the reason I bought it. I saw it displayed and right away thought of you and how much you like lighthouses." He pretended to focus on the small white beacon held lovingly in her hands.

He should've known his sister wouldn't ignore such a comment from him.

"So...tell me about this cashier." She let the lighthouse rest in her lap and placed her hands on the arms of her wheelchair.

"I shouldn't have made that comment. She was nice and yes, she was pretty. But I don't know anything about her. Except her name." He chuckled, then gestured to the figurine. "Where would you like it to be displayed? Since it's breakable you might want to keep it on your shelf."

Avril gave a nod. "Yes, my bedroom shelf will be a good place. Thanks, brother." She lifted the small lighthouse from her lap and gently re-wrapped it in the tissue paper, then placed it back inside the gift bag. "I really like my lotions too. They both smell wonderful."

As she wheeled herself toward the hallway that led to her room, Avril paused and glanced back at her brother. "So, what's her name?" She grinned.

"Emma. And that's all I know. If I learn more, you'll be the first to know." He shook his head and watched her wheel toward her bedroom. Thomas couldn't suppress a smile and his heart swelled with love for his sister. What a blessing she still had her sense of humor and the two of them could tease each other like they'd done before the accident. *If only she could walk again, Lord. At least a little.*

~ ~ ~

Where had the week gone? The days were flying by, and Emma had gotten into a comfortable routine of working each day at her aunt's gift shop, then returning to her cottage for the evening. She enjoyed walking on the beach before supper a few days each week. The wind whipping through her hair refreshed her, even when she'd had an especially busy day at the shop. It was also a relief to be somewhere and not worry about constantly looking over her shoulder.

To her disappointment Thomas hadn't been back, even though he'd mentioned he would stop in again. But she didn't know his schedule so maybe his work had taken him elsewhere. To her dismay that thought didn't sit well with her.

Her cell phone rang, lifting her spirits when she saw Molly's number. She and her best friend from South Georgia hadn't chatted in a few weeks—too long.

"Hey girlfriend. I'm glad you haven't forgotten about me since I moved." It hit her just how much she'd missed hanging out with her best friend, even though Molly was now married and hoping to have children before long.

"I could never forget you. Remember what I told you when we were in high school? You're my best friend for life, so that means you're stuck with me forever. No matter where you move, because you know I'll always live right here in Westville." Molly laughed, her voice causing Emma to yearn for home. But Coastal Breeze was her home now—at least for the time being.

"So, get me caught up. How's married life? Are you still working at the diner?" Emma was hungry for news from her hometown, and for the next twenty minutes, drank up all the tidbits her friend shared with her. News of who was getting married, who'd had a baby, and even the remodeling of Mr. Cuthbert's gas station were all interesting to Emma and helped her feel connected to her former town.

"But I want to hear about your life. Tell me about working in your aunt's gift shop. And what's it like to live so close to the ocean? I'd probably play hooky from work and hang out at the beach every day." Molly giggled, then added. "Nah, I've got too much of a guilty conscience for that, but it would be tempting." Both women laughed.

As she shared with her friend, Emma had to be careful not to mention the handsome customer. She knew that Molly would make something out of it, and there was nothing to make. Even if Thomas did stop by the gift shop again, he might be coming in to purchase a gift for a girlfriend, which was likely who the other gifts were for.

Before their call ended, Molly promised she'd come visit before too long.

"Remember, Emma Jean, just because I'm married now, that doesn't affect our friendship. You're still my bestie and always will be."

For a few seconds Emma remained silent, afraid her voice might tremble and alarm her friend. Why was she so emotional? At least Molly had lightened the mood a bit by calling her the name most of Emma's relatives had used over the years—always adding her middle name.

She cleared her throat. "Thanks, Molly. You're my bestie too, and I'm going to hold you to that visit. My cottage is small, but I've got room for a guest. Especially my best friend."

The two women chatted a few more minutes before the call ended. As Emma ate her supper and then took a quick walk on the beach before dusk, her thoughts returned to Thomas and wondered if he would in fact stop by the gift shop again. Well, if he did and if they possibly became friends, then she'd tell Molly about him. But those were mighty big "ifs," and she'd be better off not thinking about the handsome man at all.

That Sunday Emma attended Aunt Ginny's church. The couple of times she'd been, the congregation had been warm and welcoming, always encouraging her to come back. To her amusement, Midge was one of the first to rush up and greet her as if they were old friends.

The kind, elderly customer Emma had assisted in the gift shop was apparently more of a social butterfly than Aunt Ginny.

On Monday morning, while she headed to the shop, Emma thought about various people she'd met at church the day before and hoped she wouldn't have trouble recalling names if any of them stopped in the shop.

"Good morning, my popular niece." Ginny greeted her with a playful smile and a twinkle in her blue eyes. "You were quite the hit at church yesterday. And you may as well know that dear Midge is already trying her best to find a suitable young man for you, so be forewarned." She cackled, then said, "Midge really has a good heart and means well, but sometimes, she can be a bit…overbearing. But she has good intentions."

"Thanks for the heads-up. And no disrespect to Midge, but I didn't notice an abundance of young men in your church. The few I saw were with their wives and had small children with them."

Her aunt shook her head as she lifted out several gift items from their boxes. "No, there aren't many at all, but if there's even one, then Midge will try to play matchmaker. So just be prepared, and if she tries to get you together with someone who doesn't appeal to you, then you can nicely let her know. If nothing else, you can always use me for your excuse."

As Emma looked at her aunt with a puzzled expression, Ginny explained. "You could say that I need you to do some extra work for me here in the gift shop. Or even that I need you to accompany me somewhere. Then, to make sure you were telling the truth, I'll follow through with whatever you had to say. After all, I've always got some tasks to do here in the shop, and if you have to say that you're going somewhere with me, then so be it. We could head to Destin for lunch and some sightseeing. Then neither one of us would be telling a fib." Ginny laughed.

Emma shook her head and giggled at her aunt. The more she was around her, the closer she felt to her kindhearted relative. "Thanks, and I'll keep that in mind and try to be prepared in case Midge does play matchmaker."

"If you don't mind I need to tackle some paperwork today in the supply room, so I'll need you to handle the shop and customers. But if there's a problem, just holler and I'll come out to help."

Emma assured her she should be fine. "Besides, I need to get used to running it by myself for the days when you're away for a while."

Thirty minutes later Emma rang up a small sale for a local resident, then dusted shelves and organized some greeting cards. About eleven o'clock the door opened, and she glanced up, almost dropping the birthday cards she held. The handsome man from Alabama had come back!

"Hello. How are you?" Trying to sound calm and relaxed even as her heart pounded, Emma smiled at Thomas. She quickly stuck the cards she'd been holding in a slot, making a mental note to place them correctly after he left.

He wore a sheepish grin, giving the appearance of a little boy who'd been caught sneaking a cookie. "I'm good, Emma. How are you?" He ambled toward her, and a clean, woodsy scent drifted to her nose.

"I'm fine, thanks. Are you looking for anything in particular today?" A sense of awkwardness took over her, and she regretted not holding on to those greeting cards. At least that would've given her something to do with her hands. She clasped them behind her back, curious as to his reason for stopping in.

"Well, I need something for my mother. When I was here last time I bought my sister some gifts, so on this business trip I need to get something for my mom."

"That's a nice thing for you to do. Did you want to look around or do you need me to help you find something? As you can see, we're not terribly busy today." She gestured toward the center of the shop. Except for Thomas, no one else had entered the store since the previous customer left.

"I guess I timed it just right then. But I don't want to keep you from doing something else." He took another step toward her, his eyes showing a hint of anticipation.

"Oh no, you're not keeping me from anything. I was organizing some cards when you came in, and that's nothing urgent. But I promise I'm not a pushy salesperson, so if you'd prefer to look around, it's fine. It's up to you."

He appeared to be thinking about it. "Okay, I'll look for a few minutes. If you'll point me in the direction of books. You know, like small inspirational ones. I thought I saw some when I was in here before."

Emma nodded and led the way to the small section with gift books. "Here you go. There's not a huge amount, but maybe you'll find something your mom would like. If you need me to help search for a particular title or author let me know."

"Okay, thanks." Thomas leaned down to start looking at the lower shelves, so Emma headed back to the front counter, hoping she wouldn't be bombarded with customers. She straightened some items inside the glass counter, keeping her ears alert in case Thomas needed her assistance. Perhaps it was best if he didn't, because she'd have to stand close to him in the book area, and no doubt he'd hear her thumping heart.

A few minutes later he sauntered to the counter, grinning proudly as if he'd located a prize. He held up two small books—one on having faith and the other, an amusing collection of humorous short stories written especially for middle-aged women.

"I think she'll love these, and I'm pretty certain she doesn't already have them." Thomas placed the books on the counter, then tugged his wallet from a back pocket.

"Great. I'm so glad you found something, and I hope your mom will enjoy both of these."

Emma rang up the books, placed them in a bag, and thanked him for shopping at her aunt's gift shop. At that moment footsteps sounded as Ginny walked toward them, grinning from ear to ear.

"I thought I heard voices, and I was sure my niece wasn't talking to herself. At least I hoped she wasn't." Ginny chuckled and approached Thomas. "Welcome to Ginny's Treasures from the Sea." She abruptly stopped and tilted her head a bit, as if a thought had occurred to her at that moment. "Wait a minute, I've met you. Weren't you in here not long ago?"

"Yes, ma'am. I stopped in last week and bought some gifts for my sister. So today I decided I'd better get something for my mom." He gestured toward the bag he held in his hand.

"Smart man." Ginny laughed, then continued. "I'm glad you found something, and I do hope you'll stop in here again. Do you live in this area?"

As Thomas explained he lived in Alabama but worked along the Florida panhandle, Emma watched the interaction between her aunt and the good-looking man across the counter. Tempted to step out from behind the glass counter, Emma remained where she was. At least she could lean her hands on the glass and didn't feel awkward as she had earlier.

"Well, thank you again, Emma. Nice to see you, Ginny. I'm sure I'll be stopping in again, especially now that I've been given more work responsibilities in this area." He shot a grin at Emma, nodded at her aunt, and headed out the door to his car.

Emma's heart was still racing and she realized her aunt was eyeing her with a questioning expression.

"Hmm…are you attracted to him, Emma Jean? He sure is a nice-looking young man, in my opinion. Of course, I'm old enough to be his mother." Ginny stepped over to the counter only two feet away from her niece.

"Seriously, I think he is attracted to you." Her aunt hesitated, as if to gauge her reaction before continuing. "I'm a pretty good judge of character and also pretty good at reading people's feelings. And in the brief time I watched the two of you, I can tell he's interested." Ginny's lips pursed together.

Emma blew out a breath and tucked her hair behind her ears. Unsure what to say, she shrugged. When her aunt remained silent, Emma knew she needed to respond. But as much as she loved Ginny, there was no way she was going to admit to her aunt that she found Thomas attractive. Besides, there were no guarantees he'd even stop by the gift shop again, and then what? She'd feel like a fool if she had already admitted that she did in fact find Thomas Wilton attractive.

"You're kind to boost me like this. But I'm not so sure he's attracted to me. Maybe he's just a nice, polite southern man." Emma grabbed the small feather duster in a cabinet underneath the counter, then pretended to focus on dusting some items in the display.

"All I can say is I'm not trying to boost you, sweetheart. You're a beautiful young lady and Thomas's eyes revealed he does indeed appreciate your beauty." Ginny reached across the counter and patted the hand that wasn't clutching the feather duster. "I'm going back to the supply room and continue my paperwork, but you yell if you need me."

As Emma finished dusting and moved to the

greeting card area to finish her earlier task, her mind echoed with her aunt's words. Could Ginny be right? Did Thomas find her attractive? Time would tell. But there was no way she'd pine after any man again. She had learned her lesson the hard way with BG, and she wasn't about to make that mistake again.

~ ~ ~

Thomas clicked his cell phone shut and released a pent-up sigh. The aroma of char-grilled hamburgers drifted to his nose and his stomach growled. Since he was parked in the customer lot of a fast-food burger place, he may as well grab lunch.

When Mr. Chandler had phoned him fifteen minutes earlier, Thomas had done his customary procedure of pulling off the road to talk. Fortunately, he was in an area with quite a few businesses, so it hadn't been a problem to enter a parking lot.

I need some food, then I'll digest what my boss said. He got out of his car, stretched his legs, and entered the small eatery. The young girl behind the counter appeared eager to take his order, and he couldn't help noticing that she eyed him more than once. *Must be because I'm dressed in my business clothes.* He felt sure most of the customers in this coastal area dressed casually.

After getting his food, he decided to eat his lunch in the car. Besides, he could think more clearly about what Mr. Chandler had suggested. As he ate the burger and fries, Thomas replayed the earlier phone conversation. The bottom line was his boss wanted him to take an apartment somewhere along the Florida panhandle, preferably in the Coastal Breeze area, since that community was in the center of his new district.

As he finished his lunch and took another swig of lemonade, Thomas jumped as his phone rang. Surely Mr. Chandler wasn't phoning him again with another suggestion? Or perhaps trying to convince him that living in Coastal Breeze was imperative to his doing a good job and performing his duties?

When he grabbed his phone, Thomas was relieved to hear his mother's voice.

"Hello, dear. Am I interrupting a business meeting or anything important?" Bless his mother's heart—she always thought to ask if she was calling at an inconvenient time and she seemed to respect his job duties.

He chuckled, glad it was his mother and not his boss. "No, Mom. Your timing is perfect, because I've just finished my lunch and I'm sitting in my car mulling something over. My big boss, Mr. Chandler, phoned me earlier and suggested I take an apartment in Coastal Breeze, since that town is in the center of my new business territory. His reasoning is that I won't have to spend so much time driving back and forth from the Florida panhandle to our home in Alabama." He sighed, now wishing he'd eaten a salad rather than a hamburger and greasy fries.

"Well, what's the problem? I thought you'd mentioned that Coastal Breeze and some of those other communities are very quaint and appealing."

"Yes, they are. Some of the areas are more touristy than others, but overall I like the panhandle, and of course, the water is beautiful." He paused, hoping to word his concerns carefully. "I worry about Avril, and feel I need to at least be home for a little while each day to help check on her."

When a few moments of silence hung in the air, Thomas was beginning to think their call had been cut off. But then his mother cleared her throat and spoke gently.

"It's been three years. Avril has adjusted and is still trying to be more independent. You know she adores you and is always glad to see you, as am I. But you're thirty years old and have an excellent job with a thriving company. You've got to think about yourself and your future. You'd still see your sister and me, but if it would be easier and you could do a better job for your company by living in that area, then that's what you should do. Besides, I'm cutting back on my work hours, which is what I phoned to tell you." She chuckled before continuing. "Anyway, I'm here with Avril, and it's not as if she needs a full-time caregiver. She's told me that she doesn't want to be a burden to anyone, least of all her family." His mother's voice cracked, and Thomas fought the tears building behind his eyes.

He attempted to keep his tone steady. "She could never be a burden." A lump had formed in his throat and he gripped the phone tightly.

"I know, son, and I agree. That's exactly what I told her when she said that." His mother paused, then drew in a breath and spoke in a more determined voice. "Anyway, you pray about this situation and what your boss wants you to do. I'll pray also, and we won't mention anything to your sister until everything is final. Thomas, you need to think about your life. You don't want to wake up one day and realize you're old and all alone."

He thanked his mother and promised her that he would consider her words. They chatted a few more minutes, and Thomas was careful to not slip up and mention the books he'd purchased for her in the gift shop.

After the call ended he sat very still as he allowed his mother's comments to sink in. *You don't want to wake up one day and realize you're old and all alone.* She'd never spoken anything like that to him before, and he was certain the only reason she'd said that today was because of her love and concern for him. But deep down inside, he knew his mother was right. Just look at how the time had flown since he'd been an adult. Sometimes he couldn't believe he was already thirty.

Okay, so he'd pray and give it serious thought. And maybe it wouldn't be a bad idea to go ahead and scope out apartments or small houses to rent in the Coastal Breeze area. How amazing it would be if he ended up living not far from a certain gift shop employee.

~ ~ ~

What a relief to finally have her headache pain ease up. All morning Emma had been plagued with the throbbing pain, and she was certain it was due to not sleeping well, thanks to having a nightmare about drug dealers chasing BG. She'd not had a nightmare in a while, and she prayed the horrible dreams wouldn't continue. At least she could finish her workday without the pain.

At that moment the door swung open and Emma glanced up, expecting to see more women coming in to browse. Instead she saw Thomas, and her heart raced. He made an attractive sight, with a mint-green shirt and khaki pants.

"Hello. Do you need another gift for your mom or sister?" She smiled, hoping he didn't hear the pounding of her heart.

He grinned and stepped closer to her. A pleasing scent reached Emma's nose, a fresh-and-clean smell, as if he'd just taken a shower.

Thomas shook his head and chuckled. "I need some suggestions, if possible."

"About a gift idea?" She was curious and knew if he mentioned a girlfriend, her heart would plummet.

Again he shook his head. "No, sorry, but this time I didn't stop in to buy a gift. But if it would be rude if I didn't, then I'll purchase something." The playful gaze in his eyes sent her insides doing somersaults.

Emma giggled, feeling breathless. She had to rein in these crazy emotions. After all, she still knew very little about this man standing before her. "No, it's definitely not rude to stop by and not purchase a thing. Just ask my aunt. We have plenty of people who want to browse but not buy, and that's okay." She felt heat creeping up her face that had nothing to do with the warm April sunshine outside.

"Whew." He laughed, then became serious. "I stopped in to ask if you or your aunt know of any decent apartments in Coastal Breeze, or maybe someone with a small house to rent?" His dark eyes searched her face for her reply.

"Aunt Ginny might be able to advise you on that. Since I'm new to Coastal Breeze, I'm still learning my way around the area. Even though it's a small community, there's more here than I'd first thought." She smiled up at him, aware of how tall he was as he stood so close. "I'll get my aunt from the supply room." Before Emma took five steps her aunt came out of the back and approached her, a curious gaze on her face.

"Aunt Ginny, Thomas stopped in to see if we might know of a good apartment or small house for rent in Coastal Breeze. I told him you might know of something."

Ginny's eyes twinkled and her eyebrows raised. "Oh? Are you thinking of moving to our lovely little area?"

He nodded. "The truth is, my boss wants me to relocate to this area because Coastal Breeze is a central location for my district. He feels that it would be in my best interest to spend less time traveling back and forth, and then I could have more time—and energy—for my job duties. Right now, I spend a good amount of time driving to and from my home in the Montgomery area. It's never been a problem, but I recently was given a..."

His voice trailed off briefly as if embarrassed, but then he finished his sentence. "I was given a promotion, so in addition to having more territory, I also have more responsibilities." He stopped speaking as if he might've said too much.

"A promotion? Why that's wonderful for you. Congratulations." Ginny beamed at him, joined by a smiling Emma.

He ducked his head briefly and gave them both a sheepish grin. "Thank you. It was a surprise and I'm very honored. Of course, now I'll need to work extra hard so my boss doesn't regret his decision." He laughed, and the sound sent tingles racing through Emma.

At that moment the shop door opened and two women from church entered. Ginny waved at them, and then turned her attention back to Thomas.

"I tell you what. Let me ask around and see if I can find out about a small house. The only apartments in our town are the Oceanside Apartments, and I'm sure they're okay, but they are fairly old." Ginny tapped her bottom lip with a finger as she concentrated. Then she looked up at him. "If you could stop by here again within the week, I should be able to give you more information. Just give me a couple of days if you can." She smiled up at him, then flicked her gaze over to her niece.

He beamed. "That would be great. Thanks so much, and I'll be back in a few days." He'd been directing his comments and gaze at Ginny, but then as she scurried to greet her friends, he focused his attention on Emma.

"Wow, I sure appreciate your aunt helping me out. I hope she won't go to any trouble."

Emma shook her head and fingered the seashell necklace she wore. "No, I'm sure it won't be trouble for her. Aunt Ginny is a social butterfly, so she'll be tickled to have a good reason to contact folks in her church."

She giggled. "I'd go so far as to say that if anyone in Coastal Breeze could locate a house for you, it would be my aunt."

"That's good to know. I'd better get back on the road and finish my work. I have another stop today, and then will head back home to Alabama. Thanks again for asking your aunt about helping me." His eyes lingered on her face.

"No problem. Have a safe drive back to Alabama." She smiled and then pretended to busy herself with straightening the counter as he headed toward the door. Yet her eyes followed him after he exited the store. She watched the tall, handsome man stride toward his car and had a feeling her heart was in trouble. Big trouble.

PATTI JO MOORE

3

Thomas hadn't told Avril he was looking into renting a place in Coastal Breeze, and he dreaded doing so. Yet his mother had assured him that his sister would handle it fine. Besides, his mother had already reduced her working hours at the law firm where she'd worked for the past ten years, and Avril seemed to be getting more independent. So what was the problem? Why was he nervous about telling his sister that he wouldn't be home nearly as much? *Because I still feel responsible for what happened to her.*

Even after three years he carried the burden of guilt. Regardless that his mother had told him numerous times he wasn't to blame, in his mind he *was* to blame. Now Avril was in a wheelchair and most likely would be for the rest of her life. The guilt stabbed him yet again. His phone rang—a welcome reprieve from the overwhelming thoughts of his sister's situation.

Hearing Mr. Chandler's voice, Thomas knew he needed to pull off the road. Whatever his boss was calling him about would require his full, undivided attention. To his relief, there was a gas station up ahead on the right side of the road, so he could pull in and continue the phone call.

"How are things going in the Florida panhandle this week? Any major changes or updates I need to know about?" His boss had a knack for sounding professional and pleasant at the same time, which was another thing Thomas liked about the man. He could be all business, yet show a personal side too.

Thomas cleared his throat and replied, hoping to sound calm and confident. "No major happenings, but I have had several productive talks with clients in the Fort Walton area, and today I have two appointments scheduled in Destin." He wasn't sure if his boss wanted specific details or was checking to make sure his new position was going smoothly.

"Sounds good. I knew you were the right one to take over the panhandle district. Just make sure you don't let it overwhelm you, and don't ever be afraid or too proud to ask for help."

"Yes, sir. I appreciate that, Mr. Chandler."

"Remember, you can call me Mac. I would prefer that." His boss laughed, and Thomas joined in, even though he felt awkward.

Mac Chandler talked a few more minutes, mentioning the local weather in Charleston and an upcoming fishing trip. "Do you ever fish, Thomas?"

"No sir. I haven't fished since I was a kid." He

chuckled as a distant memory formed in his mind. His uncle had taken him to a local lake, and Thomas had been so proud of the two, small fish he'd caught.

"Now that you'll be spending most of your time along part of Florida's coast, maybe you'll be able to take up fishing. It's a good way to relax."

Thomas appreciated his boss's suggestion, but hoped it wasn't a warning that his new position would be overly stressful.

After the call ended, he glanced at his watch and knew he needed to get on the road. He would have just enough time to drive to his first client's appointment and not have to rush in at the last minute. He hoped these two meetings would go smoothly so he wouldn't be so late driving back home to Alabama.

It occurred to him that maybe his life *would* be simpler if he lived in Coastal Breeze. He'd save countless hours of driving time, not to mention less wear and tear on his car—and his nerves when traffic was heavy. In his free moments, he might be able to enjoy a little time on the beach—with a certain gift shop employee.

That last thought brought a smile to his face, and he decided he'd better start preparing to make the move from his Alabama home to the Florida coast.

~ ~ ~

"Emma Jean, guess what I found out today?" Ginny breezed in the gift shop door after leaving to "run a couple of errands," as she'd told her niece.

Even though Emma had thought nothing of it

and was happy to run the shop in her aunt's hour-long absence, now she was curious about those errands. Before she could reply, Ginny answered, "I think I've found a small house for Thomas to rent. Right here in Coastal Breeze!"

"Really? That was fast." She attempted to keep her voice level and not appear as eager as she felt. Would she see him more often if he lived in her community?

Her aunt laughed and shrugged. "When you're willing to ask around, sometimes things move quickly. Besides the fact that I've lived here a while now and know about everyone in our cozy community." She set her handbag on the counter and lifted out a small bag of fudge.

Emma recognized the logo on the bag from the candy shop located two blocks from her aunt's store. Right away the tempting chocolate aroma drifted to Emma's nose, and she had to use willpower not to ask her aunt if she could sample a small piece of her favorite candy.

Ginny must've noticed her eyeing the bag because she winked and nodded toward the counter. "Enjoy the fudge, sweetie. It's all yours because I ate enough this past Christmas to hold me all year, I do believe." She shook her head and giggled, then continued her previous topic. "So anyway, I told you I was running errands, which I did. I needed to get stamps at the Post Office, and I'd already planned to surprise you with some fudge. I would've gotten a bigger bag, but it's so rich, I didn't want you to get sick." She paused and lifted her handbag from the counter.

"When I stopped by the candy store, I mentioned to Cindy Lou that an acquaintance needs to find a small house to rent here in Coastal Breeze, and I asked if she knew of anyone wanting to rent out their house." Ginny moistened her lips as if about to devour a steak, then continued with her eyes twinkling. "And to my surprise, Cindy Lou said that she did know of someone. Her uncle, Mr. Grover, happens to own several small houses over on Palm Avenue, and one of his houses is about to become available. Now I know you're still learning your way around, but Palm Avenue is three streets over from where we are now." She motioned with her hands to give Emma a general idea of where the street was located.

Ginny blew out a breath and concluded her story. "Cindy Lou promised she'd talk to her uncle today and let him know that someone might be interested in renting that house. Mr. Grover will then be in touch with me, and I'll let you know what he says." A pink blush crept up her aunt's face before she trotted off to put away her handbag in the supply room.

It dawned on Emma then why her aunt had been chattering so as she relayed the details of her errands. *Mr. Grover.* Aunt Ginny was interested in the older widowed man who was active in her church. Emma had been introduced to him the first Sunday she'd attended, and now that she thought about it, her aunt had acted a bit giddy around the man. She smiled as she thought about a possible romance blossoming between the two older people. That was really sweet, and for her aunt's sake, she hoped something developed. Emma knew that Ginny had been lonely since becoming widowed five years ago.

The next day was Friday and Emma noticed a larger crowd stopping in the gift shop due to tourists arriving for the weekend. She could only imagine how the upcoming summer would be. But she was glad to stay busy and her customers were all friendly.

About one o'clock Emma finished helping a lady search for a book and she returned to the counter. The door opened and in walked Thomas. She tried not to appear overly happy to see him, yet her heart raced.

"Hi there. How's your job going?" She hoped he didn't notice her eagerness on his arrival.

He grinned and approached the counter, his familiar woodsy cologne reaching Emma's nose. "It's busy but going well, thanks for asking." He glanced around the shop. "How has business been? Looks like there's a good amount of customers." He sounded sincere and interested.

Emma gave a smiling nod. "Yes, it's going pretty well, and Aunt Ginny keeps reminding me that we'll be even busier when the peak tourist season arrives in June." She paused and grabbed the feather duster, her usual crutch. Looking up at him she continued. "In fact, the shop has done well enough this spring that my aunt is ordering some new items and extra inventory. That sounds good to me, even though I'm still learning what all is involved in running a gift shop. I'll admit there's more to it than I'd first realized." She giggled, now feeling ridiculous grasping the feather duster. She swiped at a few displayed items on the counter and then placed it back underneath.

With a grin Thomas gestured toward her hands. "Whew, I was afraid you were taking that out to whack me with it." He laughed easily and shook his head.

Emma knew her face was crimson. "No, it's just a habit, I guess. I take it out a lot just to make sure items don't get dusty with the shop door opening and closing." *Good grief, Emma, let him do the talking.*

"Well, I stopped by to see if your aunt has had a chance to ask about any places for rent in the area. If she hasn't had time to check on it, that's fine. I'm sure she has enough to do." He fingered his sunglasses as if a tiny bit apprehensive.

Just then Ginny's footsteps sounded as she approached from the rear of the shop. She waved at several customers she passed while heading toward Emma and Thomas.

"Hello there. Good to see you again." She stepped closer to him and lightly touched his arm in a friendly gesture. "I have some news that might be of interest to you." She winked.

"Really? I was asking Emma if you'd had a chance to ask around about a place for rent. But I told her I understand if you haven't."

Ginny explained about asking the candy shop owner if she knew of an available place for rent. "And would you believe that her uncle, Mr. Grover, happens to have a house that he's wanting to rent?" She laughed. "Now I'll tell you the truth, Thomas. I don't know anything about the house, but knowing Mr. Grover from church and in the community, I feel certain the place isn't a dump. But you'd have to look for yourself and see what you think. I can give you his contact information, if you'd like."

Thomas appeared pleased and relieved to hear this news. "Thank you so much. I appreciate your help more than you know, and I'll be looking into this right away." He paused as if wanting to say more, but unsure if he should. Then he blew out a breath and continued. "As a matter of fact, just yesterday my boss phoned me and encouraged me again to find a place in this area—at least temporarily. So, I'm very grateful for your help." He smiled and nodded at Ginny, then turned back to Emma.

Ginny disappeared into the supply room.

Before Emma and Thomas had a chance to visit, a customer asked Emma for her opinion on some earrings, and then Ginny returned with a smile, handing a small paper with the phone number to Thomas.

"Guess I'd better be heading back to Alabama now, but I'll be contacting Mr. Grover soon. Have a nice weekend, and I'll stop in next week." He nodded again at Ginny, then his eyes lingered on Emma before heading out the door.

The two women watched him leave.

"Such a nice, young man. And he's still single too." Ginny winked at Emma, then scurried away to check on a few customers mingling throughout the shop.

Emma was glad her aunt had stepped away

because her face was burning. Yes, there was no doubt Thomas Wilton was a very nice man, and she was puzzled as to why he was still single. Maybe he'd had a bad experience in his past just as she'd had in her life.

But she couldn't deny the thought that Thomas moving to Coastal Breeze gave her heart a lift. A very big lift.

~ ~ ~

"Avril, don't worry. I'll still see you a good bit and check on you." Thomas had finally told his sister about his plans to rent a place in Coastal Breeze, and he'd been more than a little relieved that she'd taken the news well. Maybe his mother had been right in saying that Avril was becoming more independent and Thomas needed to focus on his own life and future. But that would be a difficult challenge because of the responsibility he still felt for her. And the guilt. That painful reminder didn't have the opportunity to overtake his thoughts because at that moment his cell phone rang. A quick look at his caller ID showed his buddy's name. "Hi, Paul. What's going on?" He was always glad to hear from his high school buddy who'd remained a faithful friend to him over the years, despite getting married and having a child.

"I wasn't sure I'd catch you or not, now that you're the busy traveling professional." Paul's good-natured chuckle followed his teasing comment. "Listen, we've talked on the phone a good bit, but we haven't gone to play tennis or been to eat pizza or anything like that. Are you free tonight? I know it's Saturday and you might have plans, but if not, let's hang out."

Pleased that his married friend wanted to spend time with him, Thomas couldn't resist some teasing of his own. "Hm, let's see if I can squeeze you into my social calendar." Both men laughed. "No, seriously, that sounds great Paul. Are you sure it's okay with your wife? I don't want to be the cause of any arguments if she wanted you to stay home or watch the baby." He couldn't help a twinge of envy as he spoke those words. Even though he was genuinely happy for his friend, there were many times that Thomas thought about Paul's life and yearned to have that life too. Happily married with a child and hoping for more in the future. Even though that hadn't happened yet didn't mean it never would. *But you still feel responsible for Avril. How would that work?* The nagging reminder of his priority frustrated him, and he didn't want his private thoughts to be reflected in his tone. He shoved away any negative thoughts and focused on Paul, who was replying to his question.

"Nah, she's good with it. We've worked out a little arrangement that our Sunday School teacher suggested to all the couples in our class. Once a month I watch the baby while Meg goes out with her girlfriends—they usually go to eat or shop." He laughed, then continued. "And then she gives me her blessing to either hang out with a buddy or go look around the sporting goods store by myself. Real exciting life, huh?" Paul cackled.

Little did he know Thomas thought his life sounded ideal. "That must work out great for you and Meg. How's the baby doing?"

"He's great. I can't wait to teach him to play baseball when he's older." Paul hesitated, and then made a comment that caught Thomas completely off guard. "Hey man, you need to hurry up and marry so you can have a kid. Then our children could play together—wouldn't that be cool?" Although Paul added a chuckle, his underlying tone let Thomas know his friend was serious.

"Yeah, well, give me a little more time." Thomas hurried to change the conversation back to meeting that evening. "So you decide about this evening. Out to eat, movie, or whatever you'd like is good with me."

"Great! How about our old favorite—the Steak Palace?"

Thomas laughed, trying to remember the last time he'd eaten there. "Sure, sounds good to me." The two men discussed the time they'd meet, and the call ended.

"Does my big brother have plans on a Saturday night?" Avril wheeled into the kitchen and grinned at him. She appeared eager to hear details, so Thomas told her about the call from Paul and their supper plans for that evening.

"I'm glad you're doing something fun. Maybe one of these days you'll have a date." She looked at him with teasing eyes, but then turned serious. "You really should start dating again."

He sauntered over to her wheelchair and patted her shoulder. "Thanks for your concern, little sis. But I'm fine—I promise. I'm not over the hill yet." He chuckled and was relieved to see her grin.

"Maybe not, but you're not a kid either." She

shook her head at him and wheeled to the counter to reach for an apple from the fruit bowl.

"Thanks for the reminder." He grinned, then turned to her before leaving the room. "And I promise that if—I mean *when*—I start dating again you'll be the first to know. After the girl, of course." He winked and was tickled to see Avril giggling as she prepared to bite into her apple.

On Monday morning Thomas phoned Mr. Grover, annoyed with himself for feeling nervous about making the move to the Florida coast. After all, it wasn't forever. But then again, he felt a sense of relief after talking with the older man for about ten minutes and was now eager to take a look at the small rental house.

Since he didn't need to be in Coastal Breeze to meet with Mr. Grover until the next day, Thomas worked from home on Monday. In between doing work he tried to spend extra time with Avril, without being obvious. He knew she'd become suspicious of his motives if he kept popping into her room too often. Yet for his peace of mind, he had to make certain she knew he wasn't deserting her.

"What are you working on, little sis?" He ambled into her room after lunch, curious to see what had kept her so preoccupied that day.

She glanced up with a shy grin. "Promise you won't laugh?"

"Would I ever laugh at you?" He teasingly asked and winked.

"Humph." She feigned an aggravated expression on her face, then smiled. "This is what I've been doing. You know I love lighthouses, and after you brought me that figurine I decided maybe I should try drawing some." Her hand trembled as she held up the sketchpad so he could look.

Thomas was taken aback. "Wow, Avril. These are great." He took the drawing pad from her hands to take a closer look. Studying each carefully-drawn lighthouse, he was amazed. He knew his sister possessed some artistic talent, but he'd had no idea she was capable of drawing so well. Especially since her accident, the slightest movement took so much effort. "Sis, these are amazing. Seriously."

She fidgeted with her pencil, then placed it on her lap tray and tugged at a strand of hair.

Thomas recognized the signs when his sister was embarrassed, and she clearly was at the moment. Even though he didn't want to make her uncomfortable, he had to let her know his praise was sincere.

He nodded and placed the sketchpad back on her tray. "I promise I'm not just saying this because I'm your brother. I really had no idea you could draw like this."

She shrugged, avoiding his gaze. Still feeling embarrassed, he knew.

"I'd better get back to work at my computer. I just wanted to see what you were doing. But seriously, sis, if this is something you enjoy you need to keep at it. I'm not an art expert, but it's obvious you've got some real talent." He turned and ambled back to his room to finish his work. Yet now he had trouble staying focused because his mind whirled with ideas for his sister. Even if she only drew as a hobby, that was a good outlet for her. But after seeing the lighthouses she'd drawn, Thomas couldn't help wondering if there was something she might even do to make a little money. That would really give her a boost. He remembered how pleased she'd been when she first began tutoring their neighbor's twins in reading. Simply the fact that she had a job and was being paid for it had given Avril a tremendous lift with her self-esteem. He and his mom had both noticed it right away. So now if she was able to sell a few of her drawings—maybe in a craft show?—surely that would boost her even more.

Thomas knew he'd do whatever he could to help and encourage her. Not only because she was his little sister, but he still felt he was the cause of her being in a wheelchair. And that tugged at his heart every day.

~ ~ ~

Emma stood at the back of the gift shop reading over the inventory sheet as if studying for a test. She was trying hard to learn all she could about her aunt's business. The bell over the door tinkled announcing the arrival of another customer, and she glanced up. Thomas.

Dressed in a light blue shirt and khakis, he entered the shop and seemed to be searching for something. Or someone. As his eyes lit on Emma, his face broke out in a wide grin.

Still clasping the inventory sheet, she hurried toward the door and stopped a few feet from him. "Hey there. How are you?"

"I'm good, thanks. The reason I stopped by was to let your aunt—and you—know that I met with Mr. Grover today and I'm going to be renting the house from him. It's small, but it's all I need. I'll move in this weekend. I really do appreciate your aunt helping me out, and Mr. Grover seemed nice." He paused a few moments before continuing. "He sure talked about your Aunt Ginny a lot."

"Oh really?"

Thomas nodded. "Yes, he kept mentioning how kind and friendly your aunt is and that if she recommends someone as a possible tenant, then he has no qualms about renting to that person. He also said he and your aunt are good friends through church, and she's a very hard worker."

"Yes, she sure is. Sounds like Mr. Grover has my aunt all figured out." Emma giggled, eager to hear what else Thomas would share.

"Anyway, I went ahead and signed the papers and will start staying there next week. It's nothing fancy, but seems to be all I need. There's one other thing Mr. Grover told me, and it kind of embarrassed me." He hesitated, making her wonder what on earth he was about to share. Her face must have shown her feelings because he burst out laughing.

"It's nothing bad, so don't worry. You just look so shocked." He touched her arm, sending sparks racing through her middle.

He cleared his throat and explained that Mr. Grover was giving him a break on the rent. "All because of your aunt. He said that since Ginny recommended me, and he's good friends with her, that would qualify me for a discounted rate. I, uh…was a little embarrassed about that because I hardly know your aunt at all, and I'm so grateful she was willing to ask around and find someone who had an available house."

Emma smiled. "It all worked out, Thomas, and I'm glad it did. I'm sure Aunt Ginny was happy to help, and I hope this will be easier with your job since you won't have to spend so much time driving."

He nodded. "Oh yeah, it sure will help. I spend one-third of my time behind the wheel of my car." He rubbed the back of his neck.

"Hello there." Ginny's voice greeted Thomas as she walked toward him with two customers close on her heels. "Emma, will you please ring up these books for these ladies?" She turned to the women and smiled. "Thanks so much for stopping in today, and I hope to see you again when you're visiting our area."

Emma turned her focus to the two customers, but part of her strained to hear what her aunt and Thomas were saying. The best she could tell, he was sharing the same information he'd given her minutes earlier. Even as she counted out the customer's change, Emma noticed her aunt gushing when Thomas mentioned Mr. Grover's comments about her.

After the customers left, Emma hurried out from behind the counter to stand closer to her aunt and Thomas. They both looked at her and smiled.

"Isn't that wonderful news that Mr. Grover is giving Thomas a discounted rate on the rental house?" Ginny fingered the seashell necklace she wore, her hands slightly shaking. Yep, she was very pleased at hearing that her friend had complimented her to Thomas.

"It sure is. I hope your move will go smoothly, Thomas. Do you have any family or friends that will be available to help you?"

He nodded. "Yes, a long-time buddy of mine named Paul is going to help. I won't have much furniture, so it shouldn't be a big hassle." He smiled again at both women. "I'd better be going now, but I wanted to stop by and thank you again for giving me Mr. Grover's information. If not for you, I guess I'd still be trying to find a place to live." He grinned and told them good-bye before heading out the door.

A customer approached Ginny to ask advice on some home décor items, so Emma returned to the supply room to grab a box of greeting cards to sort before placing them in the display stands. But as she flipped through the cards, her mind centered on a handsome man from Alabama who would soon be moving to her community. That thought thrilled her, yet scared her at the same time. What if she continued being drawn to him only to be hurt again? She knew there was no way she could go through that kind of ordeal again. Ever.

~ ~ ~

"Thomas, I'll be fine. Just because I'm in a wheelchair doesn't mean I'm helpless." Avril shot her brother a look that let him know he'd almost gone too far with his concerned comments.

"I know you're not helpless. But you know I'm the protective big brother and I want to make sure you're okay. I'm glad Mom has cut back on her hours at work so she'll be here more."

"And don't forget I still have my part-time job of tutoring. The Mason twins are still coming for reading help, and Mom said a lady at church has mentioned getting math help for her nine-year-old daughter, so there's a possibility I'll have another student." Avril smiled, and Thomas didn't miss the look of pride in her face.

He was thankful his sister was able to tutor young children, so she had a job to do several times each week. Even though she was a voracious reader and enjoyed her cross-stitch and drawing, being able to do something that helped others and offered payment had been a blessing for her. Thomas didn't let himself dwell on her condition the first year after her accident, but now and then, those painful memories crept in and the sickening feeling in his gut returned.

"That's great that you might get another child to tutor. I'll look forward to hearing some more funny stories when I come home." He grinned as he referenced antics of the Mason twins.

An hour later Paul arrived and helped load up the few pieces of furniture he was taking with him. Thomas hadn't expected to feel such a mixture of emotions and silently reminded himself he'd only be a few hours away. But the fact he wouldn't be here as often for his sister continued to tug at his heart. Yet he had to admit that a part of him was excited about living on the Florida coast. More importantly, he was hoping to become better acquainted with Emma, and that thought made his heart beat faster.

After good-bye hugs with his sister and mother, Thomas climbed into his car and Paul climbed into the small rented truck. "You're sure you don't mind driving this truck?" Thomas asked his buddy again right before leaving the Wilton home. To his relief, Paul seemed at ease behind the wheel of the vehicle. Yeah, he'd owe his friend a steak dinner—or several.

The drive was smooth and the two men stayed in sight of each other as they drove. Stopping once to eat a burger helped to break up the drive, and before he knew it, Thomas pulled his sports car into the short driveway of the freshly-painted bungalow.

"Not bad at all." After climbing out of the truck, Paul eyed the front of the small house. "You've even got shrubs here across the front which is a nice touch."

Thomas nodded. "Yeah, I think the owner has done a good job with his properties, and even though it's small, it should be fine as a temporary residence." He dug the key from his pocket. "I'll show you the inside, and then we can unload my furniture."

Since the house was small, it only took a few minutes for Thomas to give his friend the tour, as he jokingly referred to his showing of the four rooms. His mother had sent cleaners and paper towels with him, but he'd use those later after his friend returned to Alabama. While Paul was there he wanted to spend time visiting with him.

Two hours later Thomas walked Paul out to the parked truck, thanking him again for his help and reminding him that all he had to do was drop off the truck at the location where he'd picked it up. Thomas had already paid the rental fee, and Paul's brother would pick him up at the truck rental facility in Alabama.

"Thanks again, man. I couldn't have done this without you. And I was serious about those steak dinners I owe you. Let me know some weekends when you're available and we'll go eat." Thomas grinned and the two men shook hands as a parting gesture.

Just then a car slowed in front of the house, and both men looked toward it.

Thomas's heart raced as he recognized the driver of the car. Emma! What was she doing here? Did she remember this was his move-in day? He lifted a hand in greeting, even as he felt Paul's eyes going back and forth from the pretty woman in the car to Thomas.

"Is that someone you know? Man, you're really something if you've already met people here in your new town." Paul chuckled.

Thomas didn't have a chance to respond to his friend's teasing because Emma had parked in front of his house and was getting out of her car. Clasping a plate, she inched toward him.

"I didn't know you'd have company already. I baked some cookies for you and thought maybe you could use a snack. It's kind of a 'Welcome to Coastal Breeze' treat." A nervous laugh followed her words as she handed him the foil-covered plate. "They're chocolate chip cookies. I hope you like that kind." She crossed her arms as if feeling awkward.

Paul laughed. "Don't worry. Thomas likes any kind of cookies." He extended a hand to her as he introduced himself. "I went to school with Thomas and we've stayed in touch. Since he was the best man in my wedding, I figured the least I could do was help him move." Paul grinned.

Thomas clutched the plate of cookies, the aroma of chocolate teasing his nose. He'd started to introduce the pair, but after Paul took the initiative, then Emma also introduced herself.

She smiled at both men, then said she needed to be going. "I only stopped by to drop off the cookies and I wasn't even sure if you'd be here yet." She paused briefly and tucked a strand of chestnut hair behind her ear. "Nice to meet you, Paul. Thomas, I hope you get settled in and will be happy living here." She spun and hurried back to her car, leaving the sweet aroma of cookies behind her.

Paul raised an inquisitive eyebrow at Thomas before climbing up into the cab of the truck. Emma had started her car and pulled away from the curb.

"Would you like to take some of these cookies with you for the road?" Thomas lifted the plate.

"No, I'll let you enjoy the entire plate, even though I'm sure they're delicious. I was wondering why you haven't mentioned her to me. She's really pretty and seems nice. Are you planning to date her?" Paul started the truck's engine.

Thomas shrugged before briefly explaining he'd met her in the local gift shop. "I'll see how things go. And yeah, I agree with your comment about Emma being pretty. From the smell of these cookies she must be a good cook too." He grinned at his friend, thanked him again for his help, and headed into his new home.

As he munched on some cookies and drank a bottled water from his small cooler, Thomas couldn't stop thinking about Emma. Could she be interested in him romantically? The thought quickened his pulse. He was attracted to her, and the truth was he had been since the first time he laid eyes on her.

Or maybe she was simply being kind, welcoming him to the area. From her mannerisms she seemed the type of person who'd do acts of kindness on a regular basis. So different from some of the women he had dated—especially Courtney, the woman he'd been dating at the time of his sister's accident. Thomas had been so disappointed to learn how self-centered she truly was.

The remainder of that weekend he got settled in his new home. His thoughts returned to Emma often, so he decided Monday he'd stop by the gift shop to thank her for the delicious cookies. And it wouldn't hurt to try and learn more about her—maybe even ask her out for a date.

4

"Are you sure this is okay?" Thomas asked as he pulled his car into the parking spot at The Happy Fisherman restaurant on the outskirts of Coastal Breeze.

When Thomas had seen Emma earlier in the week to thank her for the cookies she'd baked, he'd also asked her out to eat on Thursday, adding that he needed restaurant suggestions. When Ginny had recommended her favorite seafood restaurant, Thomas seemed pleased to take her suggestion.

Unfastening her seatbelt, Emma grinned. "This is perfect. Aunt Ginny brought me here shortly after I moved to Coastal Breeze, and it was delicious." She didn't admit to him that her insides were quivering so much she had doubts she'd be able to eat. But to her pleasant surprise, sitting across the table from Thomas proved more relaxing than she'd expected, despite his handsome looks.

After ordering their meals, he grinned at her and arched an eyebrow. "So tell me how it was growing up on a farm? That sounds like an adventure to me." He took a sip of his iced tea.

She giggled and squeezed the lemon slice in her tea. She was thankful that their server had already brought their drinks because that gave Emma something to do with her hands. "It was an adventure at times, but mostly a lot of hard work." She released a sigh, fighting an unexpected twinge of missing her family and animals. Forcing herself to smile, she went on to give him an amusing description of the goats. "My Dad says I spoil all the farm animals, but I can't help it. I guess I've got a soft spot for animals and children." She took a sip of her tea.

Thomas eyed her and nodded. "That doesn't surprise me. Just from the brief time I've known you, I would guess you'd be that way."

When the server brought their meals, Emma bowed her head to offer a brief, silent blessing, and to her delight, noticed Thomas had done the same. Not only had he opened her car door, but the man also prayed before a meal. Such a far cry from her ex-boyfriend. But she wouldn't think of BG at all, especially the horror she had upon realizing he was involved in illicit activities.

"Tell me about your family in Alabama." Full from her seafood meal, Emma laid down her fork. Had she imagined it, or had a shadow flitted across his face?

Thomas cleared his throat and shrugged. "Not a lot to tell. I have a great mom and younger sister.

My dad passed away seven years ago, which was sad. But my mom has been amazing, and we've moved forward." He hesitated as if unsure about saying more, but then continued. "My sister Avril is in a wheelchair, but I'd love to see her walk again someday."

Feeling the need to respond but seeing the pain in his eyes, Emma chose her words carefully. "I'm so sorry. Has she always been in a wheelchair?"

He shook his head and studied his plate. In a somber tone he replied. "No, three years ago she was in a terrible accident while driving. She crossed the center line, and fortunately the driver she hit wasn't seriously injured. But Avril was very hurt." His voice cracked, and his eyes misted.

Emma felt she needed to change the topic before he completely broke down. Her heart hurt for him and even though the scene was awkward, she was filled with compassion for this man who clearly loved his sister. To her relief their server appeared at that moment.

"Would you care for dessert? We have a delicious Key Lime pie." The server smiled, unaware of the serious conversation.

Emma chuckled and politely refused. "My seafood dinner was so good, but I can't eat another bite. Thank you."

Thomas also declined and asked for the check, then after the woman walked away his gaze met Emma's. "Would you like a dessert to take with you? I'd be happy to order one to go for you." He offered a smile.

"That's very kind but I'll resist since I've still

got some fudge Aunt Ginny brought me recently." Should she mention his sister again or hope the topic changed? She didn't want him to feel upset. Thankfully, she didn't need to decide because he spoke up.

"Emma, I'm sorry I got so emotional. I don't guess you're used to guys getting teary on a date." He released a soft chuckle. "It just gets to me sometime when I think about my sister in a wheelchair and not able to walk. She used to be a cheerleader and was always on the go. But she's really amazing, and I hope that sometime you'll get to meet her." He gave her a smile even though a hint of sadness remained in his eyes.

"I'd really like that, Thomas. I'm sure you're an awesome big brother to her." Emma had intended her comment to boost him, yet now he shrugged and appeared more downcast than ever.

The server again arrived and handed him the check, so the couple rose from their seats.

On the drive back to Emma's cottage, she attempted to keep their conversation light, so she invited him to church. "I call it Aunt Ginny's church, but I guess now it's my church too. The people are really friendly and welcoming."

"I'll plan to attend before long. Thanks for the invitation. I'm heading to Alabama for the weekend so I won't be able to attend this Sunday."

They'd arrived at her cottage and he escorted her to the door. "Thanks again for my yummy dinner, and have a safe drive home this weekend." Emma smiled up at him, feeling nervous for the first time. She unlocked her door and stepped inside as he said good-bye and headed to his car.

Her date with Thomas had gone very well and she hoped this was the first of more to come. Yet a niggle of apprehension ate at her thoughts and she couldn't ignore it. Was he returning to Alabama only to see his family, or did he have a girlfriend there?

~ ~ ~

Returning to his home in Alabama the next evening, Thomas hated the fact that his emotions were at war within him. A part of him was happy about relocating to Coastal Breeze, yet his concern for his sister hung over him like a cloud. A guilt-ridden cloud, at that.

His friend Paul came over on Saturday to hang out. He'd picked up a pizza and brought it, offering Avril a slice before anyone else. It always tickled Thomas that his friend went out of his way to be kind and attentive to his sister. Paul was one of the few people who truly seemed to understand the guilt that Thomas had harbored since the accident.

"Thanks, Paul. You must've read my mind because I've been hungry for pizza." Avril grinned up at him from her wheelchair, and Paul winked at her.

"Well, anytime you're really craving it and your mom or brother aren't around, you just give me a call, and when I get off work, I'll stop by and deliver a pizza. And you won't even have to tip me." He laughed, and the others joined in, especially Avril.

"Honey, I didn't know you'd been hungry for pizza. Here I've been cooking meals like roast beef and chicken and could've just ordered a pizza." Thomas's mother got in on the fun and kidding.

Thomas had a warm feeling being back with his family and best friend, yet down inside he knew his mother had been right in her advice. He didn't need to remain living at home forever because as years went by, he'd be lonely for a companion. Not to mention the fact he'd always wanted children, and his mother had laughingly reminded him that she hoped for grandchildren one day. Now with Avril handicapped, it didn't seem likely that she'd be able to provide their mother with a grandchild.

"Hey, what planet are you on?" Paul teased him with a slight punch on the arm and a laugh. "You looked a million miles away." He reached for another slice of pizza.

Mrs. Wilton and Avril had been chatting and didn't appear to notice Paul's comment. Minutes later they'd all finished eating and only the two men remained in the kitchen, drinking their colas and talking about Paul's job and married life.

"It's really great, Thomas. You should give it a try sometime." He chuckled, then leaned closer and lowered his voice. "I wanted to ask you about the pretty friend who brought you the cookies. Any updates?" He took a swig of his soft drink.

Hoping to keep his tone casual, Thomas mentioned taking her to dinner, but attempted to focus more on details of the restaurant and how delicious his flounder meal had been.

"So….do you think you'll start dating? As in regularly?"

Thomas shrugged, even though deep inside a

voice was hollering out yes. "That would be nice. I'll have to see how things go and how time-consuming my new position is. As you know, with a promotion comes added responsibility, and I'd feel terrible planning a lot of activities with Emma, and then need to cancel due to my workload."

Paul shot him a look that said he was skeptical. "I think you can manage your workload just fine. I have a feeling you're being guarded because you still feel your main responsibility is your sister." He didn't speak in a judgmental tone, just matter-of-fact.

With a nod Thomas agreed. "Yeah, you might be right. And there's still so much about Emma that I don't know."

"Well, you didn't ask my advice, but I'll give it anyway since I'm still your best friend after all these years. I wouldn't let someone like Emma get away because from seeing her one time and what you've told me, she seems like a real catch. And what I'm hearing from the single guys I work with is there aren't an abundance of girls like her around anymore." Paul appeared serious, totally out-of-character for him, which told Thomas his friend was being sincere.

Thomas nodded and playfully punched him in the arm. "Thanks, buddy. I appreciate the advice and I know you're only looking out for me. I guess that's why we're still best buds after all these years." Both men laughed, then rose from the table to head outside to take a look at Paul's new truck.

The next day as he drove back to Coastal Breeze, Thomas replayed what his friend had said.

Maybe Paul was right and he shouldn't let Emma get away. If only he didn't continue to carry that load of guilt and responsibility for Avril. His previous girlfriend Courtney had resented the time and attention he gave his sister, so their relationship hadn't lasted long at all. What if things ended up being the same way with Emma?

Yet down inside, he couldn't imagine Emma being self-centered and selfish, unless she had a hidden side to her personality.

Okay, Lord. If it's Your will for me to date Emma, please show me the way. And please watch over Avril while I'm away from her. I still worry about her so much.

~ ~ ~

The following Tuesday afternoon, Thomas phoned Emma to say hello and see how things were going. From the look her aunt gave her, Emma realized she was grinning as they talked, but she couldn't help it. Hearing his voice gave her a lift, and at the moment the gift shop wasn't busy so she was able to talk.

"I'll admit I'm enjoying this job more than I thought I would." She giggled into the phone, and then asked how his weekend had been.

"It went really well, and my buddy Paul came over and we all shared a pizza. He goes out of his way to pay attention to my sister, and I really appreciate that."

Emma was touched by how caring he was toward his sister, and that trait only made her like him more and want to be with him more. Unfortunately, she learned he was heading to

Alabama again the next weekend. The niggle of worry started again as she wondered if he was seeing someone in his hometown.

"My mom has some minor repairs and chores that need to be done, and I'd feel terrible if she hired someone to do them when I'm capable of taking care of things."

"You're not only a good brother, you're a good son, too." She was sincere and hoped he couldn't hear the disappointment in her tone. After all, his family came first, and she had no claims on him. His next comments cheered her up.

"Listen, I'm sorry I won't be in Coastal Breeze this weekend, but the following weekend I will so maybe we can do something then. Unless you have plans, of course."

"That sounds good, Thomas. Have a safe drive and I hope you get all those chores done." She laughed, still fighting a twinge of disappointment.

After the call, she had an idea that brightened her afternoon—if it worked out. She'd phone and see if Molly was available to come and visit. The two friends had been saying they needed a girlfriends' weekend, so maybe this would work. She turned her focus back to her job when a few customers entered the shop.

As she and Ginny were closing the shop about six o'clock, her aunt grinned at her. "Are you seeing Thomas this weekend?"

She shook her head and hoped Ginny couldn't tell how disappointed she was. "No, he's going to Alabama again to do some home repairs and chores for his mother. So when I get home I'm going to contact Molly and see if she can visit."

"I hope she can. You're young and you need to be with your friends." Ginny smiled and patted her arm.

"Do you have special plans?"

Her aunt's face turned rosy, and Emma wondered why her simple question had brought that reaction. She didn't have to wait to find out, as Ginny giggled and placed a hand up to her mouth.

"Listen to me, sounding like a schoolgirl. Yes, I have plans, and I'll admit I'm looking forward to my weekend. Mr. Grover has invited me to eat with him at The Hungry Fisherman on Saturday, so that should be nice." She cast a sheepish glance at her niece.

Emma squealed. "Oh Aunt Ginny, how fun! I'm glad you're eating out with him because he seems to be a nice man."

Ginny nodded, then busied herself making certain things were all set for the following day. Emma took that as a sign not to press the conversation further about Mr. Grover, but it gave her a warm fuzzy feeling to know her aunt had a date.

An hour later Emma was excited about her own plans because to her surprise Molly said she'd be able to visit that weekend. The women agreed they'd wait and catch up on talking after Molly arrived, so as soon as the call ended Emma made a list of what she needed to do and purchase before her friend's visit. She'd bake brownies—Molly's favorite. And she'd head to the store tomorrow after work and pick up plenty of snacks and colas.

Before climbing into bed that night, Emma realized she'd gone from feeling disappointed about Thomas leaving for the weekend to being very excited about her best friend's upcoming visit. She'd have to be careful and not chatter too much about Thomas, because knowing Molly and her good intentions, she'd be planning Emma's wedding before she left on Sunday.

~ ~ ~

"I don't like this a bit, Mom. Have you talked to Avril about this? Have you reminded her of how he abandoned her when she needed him the most?" Thomas ran his hands through his hair and released an exasperated sigh. Standing in the kitchen of his Alabama home talking with his mother, he wondered if he might explode. Thankfully his sister wasn't within earshot, as one of her girlfriends had dropped by for a visit and they were sitting out front talking.

Bettie Wilton squeezed out a wet dishcloth and wiped off the kitchen counter, nodding her head. "Yes. I've talked with her, but after Devin phoned, Avril was like a different person." His mother finished cleaning the counter and turned to face her son.

Thomas scowled, wondering if perhaps he should've remained in Coastal Breeze this weekend. He hated to act so upset while talking with his mother, but the current topic was painful for him. "Like a different person in what way? Did she seem upset by hearing from him? Surely it didn't please her." He reached for his water bottle on the kitchen table and took a swig, hoping it would help calm him down, although he was doubtful.

How dare that man abandon his sister after her accident, claiming he "couldn't cope" seeing her that way. And now wanting to parade back into her life as if he'd never left her. Thomas was certain his blood pressure must be rising along with the May temperatures outside.

His mother had a puzzled expression on her face, and she shrugged. "Actually, she seemed uplifted. As if hearing from Devin had given her self-esteem a big boost." She opened the refrigerator to lift out the salad she'd prepared to accompany their spaghetti. Then she offered her son a smile. "Thomas, would you step outside and see if Macy wants to join us? She's been so sweet about visiting Avril at least once a week, and I've cooked plenty for our supper."

He nodded and headed to the front door that led to the porch. His sister's voice reached his ears as he opened the door, and he almost froze. She sounded perkier than he'd heard her in a long time, and her comments were interspersed with giggles.

"Um, sorry to interrupt you ladies. Macy, would you like to join us for supper? Our mom has cooked plenty of spaghetti, and she said if you'd like to stay and eat, that would be fine."

The blonde young woman grinned and nodded. "If your mom is sure it's no trouble, I'd love to stay. Besides, Avril has a lot more to tell me." She winked at his sister, seated in her wheelchair only two feet away from Macy.

A blush crept up Avril's face at her friend's comment, and she ducked her head. Then she looked up at her brother. "Please tell Mom that Macy is staying." Then she turned her focus back to her friend. "I'm so glad you came by today, Mace." She reached out and squeezed her friend's hand, who returned a squeeze.

Yep, no denying that Macy has been Avril's best friend. Thomas returned to the kitchen to let his mother know there would be an extra person at supper, then offered to help.

Bettie lifted the pan of garlic bread from the oven and shook her head. "Thanks for your offer, son, but I've got this. Be ready to eat in ten minutes. And please promise me you won't mention anything about Devin at the table. I like for our mealtimes to be pleasant. By the way, could you please feed Caesar?" She gave him a sweet smile before returning her focus to meal preparations.

After feeding and petting the family's cat, Thomas headed to his bedroom, which now only had one twin bed and a small table since he'd moved most of his belongings to his Florida bungalow. He tried to put the previous conversation with his mother out of his mind, yet painful memories surged through him like the gulf tide coming in on the beach near his new home.

Devin Peters had been Avril's steady boyfriend since their high school days, and she had adored him. Yet after the accident that left her severely injured for weeks and then months, he'd slowly distanced himself from Avril and her family. At the time, he'd claimed that because he was heading to college he wouldn't be able to give Avril the time and attention she needed. But later on Thomas heard through their small town's grapevine that the accident had impacted Devin so deeply he couldn't cope seeing his beloved girlfriend now handicapped and felt he had no choice but to end their relationship completely.

Thomas muttered under his breath while changing clothes. "Couldn't cope. Yeah, right. He was only thinking of himself and not my sister, who'd been a loving and devoted girlfriend to him. The creep." A niggle of guilt stabbed at his heart and he blew out a breath. He knew as a Christian it was wrong to judge, yet the way his sister's boyfriend had handled having a girlfriend who'd been seriously injured just didn't sit well with him.

Remember your own flaws. The silent voice flitted through his mind, and Thomas clenched and then unclenched his fists. His head was beginning to throb and he knew the reason. Because he continued to suppress the deep guilt he felt at causing his sister's accident, he channeled his anger and frustration in other directions. Like his sister's ex-boyfriend. Yet regardless of his own feelings of guilt, there was no denying that Devin Peters had taken the coward's way out of his relationship with Avril. After all, what young man wanted his girlfriend to be in a wheelchair?

"Thomas! Are you joining us for supper?" His mother's voice called to him, and from the chattering he knew that Avril and Macy had entered the house.

"Come and wash your hands, big brother. We've washed ours and are ready to eat." Avril and Macy were both eyeing the pot of spaghetti that sat in the middle of the table, along with a bowl of salad and a basket of hot garlic bread nearby.

The aromas wafting through the Wilton kitchen would rival an Italian restaurant. "Yum, looks and smells great, Mom." He gave his mother a gentle smile to let her know he'd calmed down after their earlier conversation.

"I hope everyone will enjoy it. Nothing fancy but a good homecooked meal." Bettie glanced at her children and their visitor. Then she looked back at her son. "Thomas, will you offer our blessing, please?"

Keeping me humble. He couldn't help seeing the irony in the situation. Moments earlier he'd been ready to punch the wall as he'd thought about his sister's ex-boyfriend, and now he was seated with family about to enjoy a delicious meal and pleasant conversation. He bowed his head and offered up a brief but heartfelt thanks for their meal, then added special thanks for his mother, sister, and Macy.

The meal and conversation all went smoothly, with Avril and Macy doing the majority of the talking. At least until dessert was served. After Mrs. Wilton placed saucers with slices of apple pie in front of each person, Macy grinned at Thomas. "I want to hear what it's like living right at the beach. Avril told me that your house is within walking distance to the ocean, and that sounds heavenly to me. I cannot imagine." Macy's eyes sparkled as she looked at him.

As everyone enjoyed their pie, Thomas gave nuggets of information about his new town between bites. "It's a nice little town. So far, the few people I've met there are really friendly and helpful, and my house is small but it's clean." He chuckled before adding. "It's called a bungalow, and it's the perfect size for one person."

"Thomas is going to take me there one weekend so I can see everything for myself." Avril smiled before taking her last bite of pie.

"Yeah, I promised her I'll take her. Mom, you can come too, and Macy, you're welcome to join the little trip too." They all laughed and joked about where everyone would sleep while visiting.

"I have to say the best thing though is the sugary-white sand and the beautiful water. Sometimes the water is an emerald green; other times it looks turquoise. Really pretty to see." He pushed his dessert plate away and finished his iced tea. "And I haven't seen them yet, but I've been told that now and then dolphins will leap out of the water close to the shore. I'm hoping to catch a glimpse of those one day."

"Dolphins? Oh wow, that would be so cool to see." Macy appeared enthralled.

Avril nodded and grinned. "Yes, when he told me about the dolphins I made him promise to schedule their appearance the weekend I'm visiting." They all laughed as Thomas shook his head.

"Somehow I don't think dolphins would pay any attention to what I requested. Even though I've always heard they're intelligent creatures." He began helping his mother clean the dishes, unable to keep thoughts of Emma from sneaking into his mind. She'd told him about seeing the dolphins leaping playfully in the surf. But he'd better focus on the present with his family or his sister would be sure to notice his thoughts were elsewhere.

Even though the girls had offered to help, his mom insisted they return to their visiting on the porch. As Thomas loaded the dishwasher, Bettie whispered in his ear. "Please don't scold your sister about Devin, even if she indicates an interest in seeing him again." She gave him a look that had pleading and sternness combined. A look he still remembered from his teen years.

"Okay, Mom. I'll choose my words carefully. But I don't want to see her get hurt again."

Thomas knew he'd have to be cautious and not upset his sister. She'd been especially sensitive and vulnerable since her accident, which made him all the more protective of her. However, he had to be certain that Devin didn't slide back into his sister's life at the risk of bolting when he realized she was still in a wheelchair. Thomas also had to be certain he controlled his temper and didn't lash out at the younger man because doing so would only hurt Avril, and he'd already caused enough pain in her life.

~ ~ ~

"Oh Molly, I enjoyed this weekend so much, and now I don't want you to go back to Westville." Emma stood at her best friend's car, saying goodbye. The weekend had flown by, and both women were hoarse from all the talking and laughing they'd done since Friday evening.

"Girlfriend, this was awesome, and I'm still so

envious of you living close to the beach. Don't you worry, I'll be back to visit you sooner rather than later. And not just to be near the beach either." Molly paused and giggled, then became serious. "No, I really have missed you, so this was great spending some uninterrupted time together. We'll keep in touch, and you be sure and keep me up-to-date on Mr. Handsome, okay?" She arched an eyebrow at Emma.

With a nod, Emma chuckled. "I love our code name for Thomas. So original." She rolled her eyes before adding. "Don't worry, I'll keep you updated, even though there most likely won't be much to tell." She shrugged. "Remember, I'm trying to be very, very careful after BG."

"I know you are, but keep in mind that BG was a true creep. Not every guy is in that same category. And from everything you've told me, it sure doesn't sound as if Mr. Handsome is a thing like your ex. By the way, I always wondered what those initials stood for. Big goon?" She burst out laughing and then sobered, adding that she didn't mean to speak ill of the deceased.

Emma couldn't suppress a giggle at her friend's comment as she explained his real name had been Bud Garrison. "But the name you suggested was more fitting." She sighed sadly, but refused to let painful, bitter memories resurface.

After another good-bye hug, Emma stood in her driveway watching her friend drive away. A sudden feeling of loneliness overwhelmed her and she battled tears. What was wrong with her? Was she homesick? Yet she genuinely loved living here in Coastal Breeze.

Deciding a quick walk on the beach might help lift her melancholy mood, Emma hurried into her cottage and changed into exercise clothes, pulled her hair into a ponytail, and headed out. She still had a little while before the sun would sink beneath the horizon, and a quick glance at the tide chart she kept on her refrigerator let her know that high tide was coming in. Still, she'd have enough sandy beach left to walk on.

The strong breezes blew in her face, and she was thankful she'd pulled her hair into a ponytail. Even so, loose strands whipped around her eyes and she had to repeatedly brush them out of her face. Once on the sand, Emma paused and breathed in the ocean air. Yes, nothing like a walk on the beach to boost one's mood.

There weren't a lot of people out walking. Mostly couples. *Of course. Isn't that typical for me? When I'm feeling lonely, that's when I'm surrounded by couples.* She wasn't feeling sorry for herself, not really. Yet tears flowed. She missed her mother, and although she was thankful her father was alive, she missed being away from him. Those feelings that crept in, along with what she'd endured from BG before his death, seemed to make her more emotional at times. The wind continued whipping around her, and Emma tasted her salty tears mingled with the salty mist from the ocean.

A voice carried on the wind, startling her. She twirled in the direction of the male voice. *Thomas!* Never imagining he'd be on the beach today, she swiped at her eyes and hoped he wouldn't notice she'd been crying.

He jogged toward her, looking ruggedly handsome in shorts and a tee shirt, his tousled hair only giving him more appeal. "Hey there. I wanted to get some exercise before dark. After being in my car a while, I get stiff." He laughed, stopping about ten feet away to catch his breath. "Okay, I'll confess. I am not a runner, so that's why I get so out of breath when I do attempt to run." He shook his head as he closed the gap between them, stopping a mere foot from her.

The wide grin that had been on his face seconds ago vanished and concern etched into his features. "Hey, ...are you okay?" He leaned closer, bringing the woodsy scent of his cologne with him. His hand reached out and gently touched her arm. He appeared to want to say more, but was hesitant.

Feeling like a fool, Emma attempted a chuckle through her sniffles. "Yes, I'm okay." Then in a futile attempt to add humor to the situation, she shrugged. "I sometimes get emotional at the beach." She'd hoped her crazy comment would make him laugh. Instead he only appeared more concerned. *Oh great, he's really going to think I'm a nut job now.*

Still appearing at a loss for words, Thomas continued gazing down at her as his hand rested gently on her arm. After what seemed like long minutes—though actually mere seconds—he spoke with genuine compassion in his tone. "Has something bad happened?"

Emma was filled with remorse for giving him the impression that tragedy had struck. She quickly shook her head, grasping at loose hairs blowing in her eyes. "Oh no, nothing has happened. I'm sorry, you must think I'm crazy." She was thankful her tears had completely stopped, and she sniffled again. "No, I was just feeling a little homesick. My best friend Molly left right before I came to the beach to walk, and I was thinking about my late mother….and thinking about my dad on our farm in South Georgia." She stopped talking and shrugged. "The next thing I knew I had tears. And then you called to me. I'm sorry."

His hand remained on her arm and he gave her a gentle squeeze. "You do not need to say you're sorry. Remember I've got a sister and a mom, so I've seen ladies cry plenty of times." He offered her a grin. "Would you like to walk by yourself, or do you mind if I join you? I got back from Alabama a little while ago and decided exercise will do me good. Especially after eating my Mom's great cooking all weekend." He laughed and patted his stomach.

With her spirits already lifted quite a bit, Emma looked up at him. "I'd love some company as I walk. Why don't you tell me about your weekend with your family?" She hoped that question had been okay to ask because she still didn't know for certain that he wasn't seeing someone in his hometown. What if he'd spent more time with a female friend than with his family? But her worries were soon forgotten as he began talking.

As she listened to him tell about his handicapped sister and her kind friend, his hard-working mother and her great cooking, and the family cat Caesar, she formed a picture in her mind of a caring family she'd like to meet. *Maybe one day.*

After viewing a gorgeous sunset over the gulf, both Emma and Thomas decided they'd better return to their homes. He insisted on walking her to the door of her cottage and squeezed her hand as they said good-bye.

As Emma showered and prepared her clothes for the coming week, she couldn't get over how much better she felt than when Molly left. And walking along the beach with Thomas, listening to him talk about his family in Alabama and catching his pleasing, woodsy scent now and then had done something amazing to her spirits. Could she be falling in love with him? The thought terrified and thrilled her, all at the same time.

5

Thomas had always heard that spur-of-the-moment activities sometimes were the best ones of all, and that had proven true for him. After returning to his bungalow on Sunday night, he kept replaying his earlier walk on the beach with Emma. When he'd arrived back in Coastal Breeze from his weekend visit with his mother and sister, he'd been so keyed up with worry about his sister's ex-boyfriend wanting to step back into her life. Mulling it over in his mind was only making him angry, so he'd decided to take a quick walk on the beach, never expecting to encounter Emma.

Of course, if he'd had any idea she was crying, he never would've approached her. When she had gazed up at him with misty eyes and remnants of tears on her pretty face, something inside him had melted. It took great willpower to resist reaching out and embracing her in a gentle hug, telling her that whatever was wrong would be okay. How could he have such a strong inclination to protect and comfort her since he didn't know her that well? Yet he couldn't deny those feelings were there.

To his relief she'd brightened and laughed as he had shared humorous stories about the antics of his family's cat. Now he wondered if perhaps the Lord had placed them together on the beach at just the right time because they both had needed a lift.

On Wednesday, Thomas stopped by the gift shop after finishing his day's assignments. He was tired from meeting with several clients and was hoping to do computer work from his bungalow the remainder of the week.

A mixture of pleasing scents greeted him upon stepping into the shop, which he assumed were from the many candles and lotions for sale. He spotted Emma right away. She assisted a thirty-something mother with two young children in tow. Keeping a distance, Thomas observed her interaction with the children and was struck by her gentleness and playful smile with the little ones. She seemed to be a natural, which made him wonder if Emma wanted children of her own someday.

At that moment she glanced up and saw him. Her smiling face brightened even more—or maybe that was wishful thinking on his part. He grinned and waved, hoping she wouldn't rush her time with the customer simply because he'd entered the store.

As soon as the woman and children exited the shop, Emma hurried out from behind the counter to join him. "Hello. Are you having a good week?" A fresh, citrusy scent drifted to his nose, and he was sure it was her cologne rather than something in the shop. It was very pleasing, and he wondered if Avril might enjoy wearing that scent too.

"Yes, I am, but it's been a busy week so far. Fortunately, I've gotten all my client appointments behind me now, so I'm hoping to work from home the remainder of this week."

Her face paled and her smile faded. "From home?"

Not understanding why his comment seemed to trouble her, he nodded. "Yes, or should I say from bungalow instead?" He laughed and was relieved to see her laughing too.

She cringed as she explained. "When you said you could work from home, I was thinking you meant your home in Alabama. And I know that's not a quick drive for you, and you'd already mentioned being tired." Her blushing face only added to her beauty.

He gave her a grinning nod. "Oh, I see now what you thought I meant. No, now when I mention home I'm referring to my cozy bungalow. Unless I also mention Alabama." He paused and shook his head. "And now I've probably confused you with my rambling. Maybe I *have* worked too much this week." He threw his head back and chuckled again. Then he remembered his reason for stopping by the shop. "I don't want to keep you from your work, but wanted to say hello and see if you have plans for this weekend. If not, I wondered if you'd enjoy joining me in a game of miniature golf. I've noticed a course off the main highway coming into Coastal

Breeze."

"Sure, that sounds great. To be honest, I haven't played in years. So I'm sure I won't be very good, but it should be fun. And hopefully we'll have good weather." She pushed her hair away from her face and smiled up at him.

He really wanted Emma to enjoy herself, especially after seeing her emerald-green eyes filled with tears on Sunday. The image of her tear-streaked face had entered his thoughts more than a few times since then, so he hoped doing something fun would give her a lift.

"Okay, sounds great. Afterward we can go eat, if that suits you. And on Sunday morning I plan to finally visit the Coastal Breeze Church, and would be happy to give you a ride." He hesitated and decided to go ahead and express his thoughts aloud. "You would be doing me a favor if you would ride to church with me." He laughed at her puzzled expression. "Since I've never visited your church before, I would feel more at ease walking into the building with someone who knows her way around. Would you mind?"

She nodded. "I'll be happy to ride with you. And I promise, it's a friendly group of people and the pastor preaches really inspiring sermons. So hopefully you'll feel right at ease as I did the first time I visited."

Just then a pair of older women approached Emma, smiling and clutching bottles of scented lotion. Since they needed to ask a question, Thomas knew he should leave. Besides, it wouldn't be long until the shop would be closing. He smiled and bade

Emma good-bye, then turned to head out the door.

As he stepped outside into the late May afternoon, the breeze blowing in from the ocean offered a soothing warmth to his face—and his spirits. He realized then how much he was looking forward to the upcoming weekend. Could this be the first of many weekends that he and Emma would spend together? He hoped so, because that thought was very appealing and even made him forget how tired he was.

~ ~ ~

Saturday morning Emma awakened with a sense of anticipation. She'd be spending much of today with Thomas and she was thrilled. Yes, no use in denying it, even to herself. She'd come to realize that the more she was around him, the more she wanted to be around him. And so far, he'd not given her any reason to think he couldn't be trusted or was keeping sordid details about his past from her.

Her happy mood was abruptly dashed, however, as a crackle of thunder sounded overhead. Even with her bedroom curtains closed, she saw the flash of lightning as it split the sky. *Oh no. No miniature golf or a walk on the beach in this weather.* So much for their fun plans. Now what? Did this mean their date was off, or would Thomas have another suggestion? Since he did some of his work on the computer from home, Emma couldn't help wondering if he'd say that due to the inclement weather he would stay home and work. Her heart sank.

She dragged herself out of bed and padded to

the kitchen, turning on the coffee pot before going to brush her teeth. A quick look out the kitchen window showed a dismal, stormy morning. Ugh.

As soon as she finished brushing her teeth and headed to the kitchen for coffee, her cell phone rang. *Thomas.*

She answered and did her best to sound upbeat, despite her mood matching the weather at the moment. "Good morning. I guess the weather report changed, huh?" She offered a wry chuckle, then cringed as thunder shook her cottage. She did not like storms—at all.

"Yeah, I guess it did. Oh well, are you still free today? If so, we'll do something else."

Her heart raced in anticipation. She was secretly relieved and almost ecstatic that he still wanted to spend time with her today rather than seeing it as an opportunity to accomplish more work.

"Sure, whatever you'd like to do is fine with me."

"Okay, how about we take my car and go see a movie over in Destin? Or we could visit some shops there, and then go out to eat." He paused, and when he spoke again his tone had a mischievous note. "Or….we could just get in my car and I'll start driving. We can see where we end up and what we'd like to do there." He laughed, the sound sending tingles coursing through Emma.

"Wow, that sounds like a real adventure. But with this stormy weather I don't think we need to go too far. Maybe heading over to the Destin area will be far enough. What do you think?" Another rumble of thunder followed her question.

"Sounds good to me. Besides, I don't enjoy driving when the roads are slick and people drive crazy, so the Destin area should be far enough. How about if I pick you up in an hour—is that okay? Or do you need more time?"

She assured him an hour would be fine and the call ended. Emma clicked off her cell and sat for a few minutes, thinking about Thomas. Would he always act this patient and kind towards her, or was he simply trying to impress her now? Without warning, painful memories of several dates with BG flitted through her mind, and she almost winced. He'd possessed a fiery temper, and often when she thought they were going to do one thing she learned he had changed his mind. It was usually his way or nothing.

Emma shook her head in an attempt to shove the bitter remnants of her past away. It did no good allowing those horrible thoughts to take hold in her mind, because all of that was over. Thankfully. If she even considered what might have happened to her while she'd dated BG, it made her feel physically sick. The thugs he was involved with would go to great lengths to get what they wanted. How could she have been so naïve? She'd had no clue at the time about his illegal activities. Her gut tightened, and she took a deep breath, offering another silent prayer that none of his accomplices knew where she'd moved.

Okay, she needed to get ready for her date with Thomas. A quick glance across the road from her bungalow showed a stormy sea, with angry waves splashing onto the shore. How nice it would be if she could take all her painful, ugly memories and toss them into the ocean to be washed away forever. But she couldn't. Yet what she could do was pray for strength to ignore those scars from the past, and also pray for strength and wisdom as she moved on with her life.

Dressing in a brightly-colored Capri outfit, applying make-up, and wearing her hair hanging loosely about her shoulders helped Emma feel somewhat better. She took one more look in the mirror before turning off her coffee pot and grabbing her handbag and umbrella. With an ear tuned to listening for Thomas's car, she didn't have to wait long.

Still being a gentleman, Thomas hurried to the front door of her cottage. As he escorted her to his car, then opened the door for her, Emma grinned up at him. "Since the weather's so nasty you didn't have to get out of your car. I was listening out for you." She slid into the seat and fastened her seat belt as he scurried around to his side and climbed in.

He looked over at her with a grin. "Oh yes, I was taught that it's polite to always go to the door for a lady. And open doors too." He chuckled and started the car's engine. "Being raised by a Southern lady ensures learning good manners." A playful wink followed his comments.

A warmth spread inside her and Emma grinned at him. "Your mother apparently did an excellent job with her teaching, because you're very polite and mannerly." Okay, was she sounding a bit cheesy here? Yet her words were sincere. She meant everything she'd said. Once again uninvited memories from past dates with BG crept into her mind. Had he ever opened the door for her? Warning bells should've sounded while she dated BG. She should've realized those signs of his uncaring attitude were not just from the lack of a good upbringing.

Stop! Emma silently scolded herself for allowing any thoughts from her painful past to interfere with her day. No, she needed to enjoy her time with him to the fullest. The rain pattered harder on the windshield, and the wipers swished back and forth, as if also scolding her for allowing negative thoughts to intrude. With their rhythm, the blades seemed to be admonishing her to think positive. She almost giggled but caught herself. Thomas would surely think her nuts.

"So....anywhere in particular you'd like to go today?" He asked the question but kept his eyes focused on the road ahead. He also maintained a slower speed on the slick roads, and Emma appreciated his careful driving.

"Oh, wherever you'd like to go. You're the driver." She chuckled, feeling thankful to be spending the day with this handsome, thoughtful man. "Seriously, it doesn't matter to me. I'm disappointed the weather didn't cooperate so we could play miniature golf as you'd suggested."

"No worries. We'll play that another time." He swerved as a pick-up truck pulled out from a side road. A frustrated sigh escaped his mouth and he shook his head. "Crazy drivers." Then he laughed.

"I sound like an elderly person complaining about teenage drivers, don't I?"

"No, you sound like a careful driver. And as your passenger I thank you." They both laughed. Yet Emma's thoughts were on his earlier comment about playing miniature golf on another date. *So that means he's planning on future dates with me.* She couldn't deny that thought made her heart sing, and at that moment she felt as if the sun was shining. At least it was inside her.

Thomas cast a quick glance over at her and asked, "What are you over there grinning about? Did you come up with a suggestion of somewhere for us to go today?"

She blushed, embarrassed he'd caught her grinning at her private thoughts. She'd have to be more careful. "I was thinking that even on rainy days people can still get out and have fun."

"Yes, you're right. And I have to confess that if we hadn't planned a date today, I'd most likely be doing work on my computer. Not that I don't enjoy my job, but everyone needs to take breaks."

Emma exclaimed. "Look, that sign ahead says there's an arcade. Would you like to stop there? Since we can't play a game outdoors, we could play some games inside the arcade. Unless you'd rather not." She almost held her breath as she awaited his response. What if he didn't enjoy those kinds of games as much as she did? Emma had fond memories of playing arcade games at the local bowling alley in her hometown.

"Sure, that sounds great to me." He turned on his blinker and eased into the parking lot. Although there were quite a few other cars, they found a parking spot not too far from the door.

Thomas hurried around to open Emma's door, and since the rain had tapered off, she didn't bother to open her umbrella. They rushed side-by-side into the arcade, greeted right away by sounds of laughter and the smell of popcorn.

People milled around from game to game, and Emma was pleased that it wasn't only teens. Several families, including grandparents, enjoyed the games and each other. Younger couples stirred memories of Emma's teen years when she often visited her local bowling alley with friends.

"Where to first? Or would you like something to eat?" Thomas squeezed her shoulder.

"How about over there?" Emma pointed to one wall that had a row of skee ball and pinball games lined up. Skee ball was her favorite game to play, although she'd probably be terrible at it now since she hadn't played in years.

"Sure." He walked beside her, then inserted coins into two games next to each other.

"I used to love this and was pretty good. But that was years ago." Giggling like a school girl, the years peeled away. She picked up a hard, wooden ball and tossed it, pleased that it didn't bounce off the side.

It didn't take long for her to fall back into the groove of playing the game, and she did better than she'd expected. From time to time, she glanced to see Thomas, and from what she could tell, he was enjoying himself.

"Have you played this game recently? Because

you're doing great." She clasped a wooden ball in her hands and grinned at him.

"Yeah, I snuck in here last night to practice, just in case you decided you wanted to come here today." He threw back his head in laughter. "No, I haven't played this in years. And to tell you the truth, I'd forgotten how fun it is."

She giggled, amused at his sense of humor.

After several more rounds of the game, they decided to try a few other games.

Before Emma realized it, two hours had gone by. Thomas glanced at his watch, then looked down at her. "You've got to be hungry by now, aren't you? I'm starving."

She nodded. The truth was she'd been hungry but had been having too much fun. Besides, she wanted him to be the one to suggest getting something to eat.

"Unless you want to stay here and eat hot dogs and popcorn, how about we head to an actual sit-down restaurant and eat?" Anticipation glimmered in his dark eyes.

"Sounds great to me." She realized she hadn't felt this happy in…she couldn't remember.

After eating at a casual, family-style seafood restaurant, complete with a table by a window that overlooked the gulf, the couple headed back to Coastal Breeze. The earlier rain had stopped, but the sky remained overcast. As they drew closer to their small town, the sky brightened and by the time Thomas drove onto Emma's street the sun was shining.

She gasped and pointed. "Look! A rainbow."

Sure enough, a beautiful rainbow arched across the sky overhead. The same sky that earlier had been gray and dismal-looking now featured an array of gorgeous colors.

"God's artwork." Emma whispered the words while observing the beauty.

Thomas craned his neck to peer through the windshield and a smile broke out across his face. "Yep, it sure is. And it's beautiful."

Neither of them spoke for a few moments as they both admired the rainbow in silence. Then Thomas reached over and squeezed her hand, sending the good kind of chills up Emma's arm.

"I think a rainbow is supposed to be a very good sign." His eyes held a warmth as he gazed at her, then slowly released her hand.

Emma wasn't sure what to say, so she offered a smiling nod in agreement. As much as she hated it, disappointment coursed through her when he'd released her hand. Such a small gesture, yet it seemed to mean so much. At least to her. Maybe he was only being nice. Or then again, maybe he was letting her know that the rainbow could mean a good sign for their relationship. She'd cling to that thought—at least for now.

~ ~ ~

The next morning Emma drove her car to Aunt Ginny's house, then both women headed to the Coastal Breeze Church. Though Thomas was going to pick her up at her house, they decided to meet in the parking lot so Emma could ride with her aunt as she usually did.

"I'll wait here in the car and watch for Thomas,

and you can go ahead and visit with your friends."

The older woman's eyes twinkled as she was about to get out of her niece's car. "Now you're sure you don't mind if I go on ahead, dear? Midge is bringing me her pound cake recipe and said she'd look for me before church starts, but if you'd rather, I can wait here with you."

Emma had the feeling her aunt was ecstatic that Thomas was visiting their church, and especially happy that her niece was going to accompany him into the building.

She reached over and patted Ginny's arm. "I promise I'm fine. Besides, he should be here any minute, and then we'll hurry inside so we don't make a grand entrance after the service has started." She laughed, trying to ignore her racing heart.

As she watched her aunt walk at a brisk pace toward the stone building, Emma couldn't help but be thankful Ginny was in such wonderful shape for her age. Emma only hoped she'd be close to being that fit and energetic at Ginny's age. A sudden tapping at her window jolted her from her thoughts, and she swiveled to see Thomas peering at her through the glass.

She opened her car door to hop out, when Thomas, as usual, offered his hand to help her climb out. Such a gentleman. And so handsome, too. Today he wore a light gray suit with a mint-green shirt that contrasted well with his dark eyes. She smiled up at him. "Good morning."

Emma read appreciation in his eyes, making her thankful she'd chosen her light blue dress for today. She'd rolled the ends of her hair so loose curls hung on her shoulders, and her dressy sandals made her feel more feminine.

"Good morning to you. I hope I'm not late." He glanced at his watch.

"Nope, you're perfect." She hadn't meant to use that word choice, but somehow it described his arrival time and the man himself. A niggle of worry prodded her mind. Would he always be so polite and caring? Almost too good to be true, and she'd never dated anyone with so many wonderful qualities. When would everything fall apart?

She had to shove away those negative thoughts and only focus on the present time. No person was perfect, and she was certain that Thomas had flaws just as she did. Yet so far he'd been wonderful, so she needed to appreciate that and enjoy their friendship.

Thomas opened the bright red door of the stone building and held it for her. An older man with a friendly face greeted them each with a bulletin.

Emma spotted her aunt right away and was relieved to see that Ginny had saved enough space for the two of them on her church pew. "We can sit with my aunt, if that's okay." She whispered behind her. He nodded, straightening his tie.

Throughout the worship service, Emma tried very hard to keep her mind and thoughts centered on the reason she was there. Yet she had to admit it was a wonderful feeling having this attractive man seated next to her, and she wondered what it would feel like to be kissed by him. She snapped her mind back to the pastor's sermon. Today he was speaking on releasing fears and worries to God, and Emma couldn't help but think how much that message applied to her. For a split second she even wondered if perhaps Aunt Ginny had urged Pastor Jack to preach that particular message, but knew she was being ridiculous. But she was thankful the minister had chosen that topic, because it was one she needed to hear.

"Wow, that was a great sermon. And the choir did a nice job with their music." Thomas commented as they stood following the ending of the service.

Emma agreed, but before she could comment further, several members of the congregation approached them to welcome Thomas. Since she'd been attending for almost two months, many of the members recognized her, but not the visitor with her.

One elderly lady whose name Emma didn't remember peered at Thomas before winking at Emma. "Oh, is this your fiancé?" The lady reached out a veined hand to clasp Thomas's hand in a hearty shake.

Inwardly cringing, Emma tried her best to appear composed as she gently corrected the well-meaning lady. "No ma'am. He's a friend. Thomas Wilton is from Alabama, and has recently moved here to Coastal Breeze." To her relief several other church members stepped up to welcome him and speak to Emma.

Ten minutes later when they headed to the parking lot, Ginny rushed up to the couple. "I forgot to tell you both that I've cooked a ham-and-potato casserole and there's plenty. Would you like to join me?" She grinned at her niece, and then up at Thomas.

"Sounds great, if you're certain there's enough." Emma cast a quick glance at Thomas, not wanting to embarrass him in case he'd rather eat something else. But she thought it was very kind of her aunt to offer.

He nodded. "Sure, if you're certain it'll be okay. But please let me stop at a store and pick up a dessert."

Ginny beamed as she reached out and squeezed his arm. "Oh my goodness, aren't you the polite one. Thank you anyway, but I've already prepared not one, but two desserts. If you'll just follow Emma's car to my house, we'll be on our way." She stopped before climbing into her niece's car. "Unless you want to ride with us, and then Emma can bring you back here to pick up your car.

The three adults climbed into Emma's car and within minutes she'd driven them to her aunt's home. As they were all about to disembark the vehicle, Ginny laughed and directed a comment to Thomas. "You see now that everything and everyone is within walking distance here in Coastal Breeze. Definitely a very small town." She smiled as he assisted her from the car.

To Emma's relief, there were no awkward moments of silence during the meal with her aunt. Conversation came easy as they finished dessert and coffee. Emma cleaned up the dishes as Ginny and Thomas remained visiting at the table. Even though he'd offered to help her—which gave her heart a leap—she had insisted that he and her aunt relax.

Ginny questioned him about his job and family, and then told him a little about Coastal Breeze.

When the couple said good-bye to the older woman later that afternoon, Ginny leaned up and gave Thomas a quick hug. He reciprocated and thanked her again for the meal. As Emma embraced her aunt in a hug, Ginny whispered in her ear. "You'd better not let him get away. He's a treasure." Then she drew back and winked at her niece.

Emma only hoped Thomas hadn't heard what her aunt had whispered, yet her pulse raced as they walked to her car for the drive back to the church.

"I had a nice time today. The church service was great, and your aunt is a wonderful cook." He said as Emma pulled into the parking spot next to his car.

"Yes, Aunt Ginny loves to have people over for meals or just for visiting. I could tell she was glad we ate with her."

He climbed out of her car, told her to have a good week, and then leaned back into the front seat. "I really enjoyed our time together this weekend, Emma. I'll be going home to Alabama next weekend, but when I'm here in Coastal Breeze, I'd love to do some more activities on the weekends, if you'd like." His eyes locked with hers, and Emma's pulse raced. For a second she thought he might lean across the seat to kiss her, but he didn't. Just as well, because with his height that might've been awkward for him.

She smiled and nodded. "Sounds good. I hope you'll have a nice week and don't work too hard."

After watching him climb into his sports coupe, she backed out to drive to her cottage. Yes, this had been a delightful weekend, and Thomas must've enjoyed it as much as she did since he'd mentioned spending more weekend time together in the future. She couldn't deny feeling disappointed that he would return to Alabama the following weekend, but she wasn't really surprised. She had a strong feeling that he was very protective of his handicapped sister, which was commendable. She only hoped that his family was the real reason he returned to Alabama, and not to see a female friend. Yet he'd given her no indication of a romantic interest in his hometown, so Emma needed to release those doubts and worries.

That night she had difficulty falling asleep and figured it was due to drinking too much of Aunt Ginny's sweet iced tea. But down inside Emma knew it was because she couldn't stop thinking about a certain man from Alabama who'd captured her heart, whether she wanted to admit it or not.

PATTI JO MOORE

6

The days were flying by and Thomas couldn't believe it was already Friday. He finished his work assignments on his computer, and then prepared to drive to Alabama, fighting a twinge of disappointment that he wouldn't be spending any of his weekend with Emma. There was no denying that he'd thoroughly enjoyed his time with her last weekend. And he was certain she felt the same way.

Before heading out the door of his bungalow, his cell phone rang. Seeing his boss's number, he answered with trepidation but attempted to keep his voice steady. Hopefully his boss was still pleased with his work.

"Thomas, it's Mac Chandler here. Are you in the middle of a meeting?"

"No, sir. What can I do for you?" There was no way he was telling his boss he was about to head home to Alabama, even though he was doing nothing wrong. He was already ahead of schedule with his work for the month of May.

"I'm glad you asked because I need you to do something very important for me." Mr. Chandler cleared his throat before continuing. "The hotel over in Watercolor—where Curtis Pettigrew is the manager—I need you to swing by there and meet with Curtis for a few minutes. I hate to ask you to go out of your way if you're not already in that area, but this is important. Curtis phoned me earlier and was concerned about some numbers not looking right...and he was quite upset. You seem to have a knack for helping our clients keep a level head, so I figured you'd be the right one to speak with him. Anyway, if you can do this, it'll be a big feather in your cap." His boss released a deep laugh, then continued. "He's expecting you before noon, if possible. No need to call his hotel, just show up."

What could he say? When he'd accepted this promotion, Thomas knew there was the possibility of impromptu meetings with clients and other items popping up that weren't on his agenda. He'd have to make the best of it and follow his boss's wishes.

"Yes, sir. I'll head to Watercolor right away. And I'll do my best with Mr. Pettigrew. The last time I met with him, everything went smoothly, so hopefully if he's upset, that will pass quickly."

"Very good. I knew I could count on you. Your attitude in this situation is one of the reasons you're in this present position. Thanks so much."

Their call ended, and Thomas blew out a breath. He changed into business clothes and then phoned his mother to explain he'd had an unexpected appointment arise. He didn't want her worrying since he'd be arriving home later than planned.

He arrived at the hotel in Watercolor around eleven, and to his relief, Mr. Pettigrew didn't seem nearly as upset as he'd expected. In fact, after Thomas addressed the business-related concerns, the client opened up to him about some personal concerns, including his wife's difficult pregnancy and the recent passing of his father. Thomas listened patiently as the man shared with him.

"Would you like me to pray with you?" Thomas asked. When he nodded, Thomas offered a brief but heartfelt prayer, then asked Mr. Pettigrew if he could do anything else to help him.

The fortyish man shook his head, and with misting eyes, peered up at Thomas. "No, thank you. You've been a tremendous help to me today. Not only did you clear up my questions about the numbers on my reports, but you sat and listened as I told you my troubles. And I know that's not part of your job description." His last comment lightened the mood, and both men chuckled. But the mood turned serious with Mr. Pettigrew's next question.

"Do you have any children, Mr. Wilton?"

"No sir, I'm not married." He wondered where this was heading.

"Well, despite the trials and traumas, such as problem pregnancies and sickness, marriage and children are well worth it. Just something to think about. Thank you again for helping me today."

Thomas shook his hand. "I'm glad I could help, Mr. Pettigrew. I've had people help me when I was burdened, so I'm more than happy to help someone else."

The other man appeared thoughtful as he digested Thomas's words. "You have a good heart. I'm going to let Mr. Chandler know what a godsend you've been to me today. And one other thing." He held up a finger as Thomas paused to look at him.

"Call me Curtis. I insist." He grinned at Thomas, who nodded and chuckled.

Minutes later Thomas climbed into his car to begin the drive to Alabama, feeling a sense of accomplishment. Curtis Pettigrew not only needed some job-related advice, but even more importantly the man needed someone to show concern about his personal burdens. And Thomas had been that man.

Even though Curtis had mentioned telling Mr. Chandler how helpful Thomas had been, he decided that what was most important was the satisfaction he'd gotten in knowing that he had helped—truly helped—another person that day. That was worth more than any company-given accolades, in his opinion.

As he pulled onto the main highway that would take him toward his Alabama home, he reflected on Curtis's comments about marriage and having children. Totally unexpected comments, but Thomas had to admit when the hotel manager had asked about marriage, only one face came into his mind. Emma Hopkins. The gentle, pretty, soft-spoken woman who inhabited many of his thoughts these days, and who he wished he could be with this weekend.

~ ~ ~

"So what's the problem? Everything sounds great to me." Molly had phoned her that weekend to see if anything new had developed with Thomas.

"I'm afraid, Molly." Emma gulped, hating the fear that still caught hold of her at times.

"Afraid of what? BG is in the past. Not only in the past—he's gone. For good." Molly's voice escalated in volume as if needing to make certain her best friend realized the creepy ex was no longer among the living.

"I know—you're right. It's just that I was so naïve when I thought BG was a decent person, and look how wrong I was. Horribly, horribly wrong." Emma shuddered even now as old memories were dredged up.

"You were younger and didn't know. You trusted him and had no idea what he was involved in. I don't like to speak ill of the deceased, but he was a real jerk. A terrible person. I'm just thankful you got away from him unharmed, except for the awful memories you still carry. But please try to let that stay in the past. As I reminded you a little while ago—that creep is gone for good. You won't ever, ever have to worry about him bothering you again." Molly paused a few seconds before asking. "Have you been bothered by any of his cronies? They don't know where you live, so you should be safe. Not that they'd have any reason to look for you."

Emma drew in a deep breath, hating to admit her fear, but knowing she could confide in her best friend. "No, but that's the other reason I'm afraid. I have this crazy fear that somehow one of them will come after me, thinking I had some connection to their dealings, which I didn't." A shudder ran through her at the thought. "I had no idea BG was involved in illicit drug dealings until his death." What a nightmare! Why had she even dated him to begin with? *Because he acted very nice and attentive at first.* The silent answer in her head was a reminder of just how naïve she'd been after meeting BG at a party.

Molly's tone was comforting. "You don't need to live in fear. Everyone knows you had absolutely nothing to do with any of BG's illegal dealings and didn't even know what he was involved in, so none of his thug friends have any reason to pursue you. Just be careful and if you ever do feel threatened or see anyone suspicious there in Coastal Breeze, go to the police pronto. But I wouldn't think you'd ever have to worry. Only your family and closest friends know where you've moved, and no one is blabbing your whereabouts to anybody."

"You're right. As usual." She added with a chuckle. Then her tone turned serious again. "I know I need to pray more about this. Pray that I'll release my awful memories and not live in fear. And also pray for guidance where Thomas is concerned because I really do like him."

"Yeah, I can tell you really like him, girlfriend. It shows." Molly giggled.

"That obvious, huh?"

"Um…yeah, pretty obvious. But that's okay, because you deserve to be happy. And as your best friend I am thrilled to see you happy. So pray about your relationship with Thomas, and I'll pray too."

The two women chatted ten more minutes, then

Molly said she needed to go. "I think I'm fighting something because I've been feeling yucky lately. I don't want to miss work because I'm saving up more time for a vacation with my hubby and more trips to see my best friend who lives in a gorgeous little beach town."

"Okay. I'll pray that you don't get the flu. Take good care of yourself, and tell your hubby I said hello."

As she put a small load of laundry in the washer, Emma's mind drifted to her father. She needed to return home to Westville before long and visit her dad and see the farm. The truth was she missed her home there. And she missed her dad. Yet she felt that living and working in Coastal Breeze was where she was supposed to be. At least for now.

A few minutes later her phone rang, and her aunt's voice came through. "Hello, dear niece. You haven't gone to bed, have you?"

Emma suppressed a laugh, not wanting to hurt her aunt's feelings. Since Ginny usually turned in early, she always assumed others did too. A quick glance at her kitchen clock showed it was only eight o'clock and Emma was going strong.

"No. I'm still awake and doing laundry."

"Okay, good. I never like to wake anyone after they've gone to bed, but you're still so young and energetic, so you probably stay up much later than I do." A nervous-sounding chuckle followed her words and Emma wondered what was going on.

"Well, no worries. You can phone me anytime, even if it's later at night. Many evenings I sit up reading until close to midnight."

Ginny spoke slowly, as if about to release some important news. "The reason I'm calling is to ask a favor of you. Now pray about it if you need to, and don't feel pressured."

Emma's heart skipped a beat. What on earth was her aunt preparing to ask? She couldn't imagine.

"Our Coastal Breeze Church is planning to have a small summer festival—most likely in early July. We've discussed having one in the past, but no one ever volunteered to take charge and get things lined up." She paused and cleared her throat. "So I told the people on the committee—yes, we've formed a small committee for such activities—that if my niece was willing to help me, I would head up our first summer festival. Since it's already May, I knew we wouldn't have time to prepare for a spring festival, but getting ready for one in the summer shouldn't be too difficult."

Ginny paused a moment before continuing. "Perhaps I shouldn't have mentioned it to the committee until I spoke with you first, but at our little meeting, the more I thought about it the more excited I became. Please forgive me if I've put you on the spot. No one—including me—would think badly of you if you say no. After all, it's your decision. As I mentioned earlier, if you need time to pray about it and think it over, that's fine. Since our church is small, this festival would be on a smaller scale, so it shouldn't involve too much work." Ginny's words tumbled out.

Yes, there was no doubt that her aunt was

tickled pink, as she would say, over the idea of heading up a summer festival. Should Emma say yes? Maybe it would be fun. On the other hand, it could involve much more work than her aunt realized. But the bottom line was that her precious aunt was asking a favor of her, and she owed it to her to comply.

After a few seconds of silence, Emma spoke. "I'll be happy to help you. All I ask is that if there's a dunking booth involved, I do not want to take part in that." She giggled and was relieved to hear her aunt chuckling.

"Not to worry, dear. At this point I'm not planning on a dunking booth—maybe next year." Her next comment caused Emma's heart to race.

"I was wondering if you think Thomas might be willing to help us—at least a little. A project such as a festival always needs men to assist in different areas. Especially a strong man like Thomas."

Oh no, was her aunt purposely looking for ways to get Emma and Thomas together more? Not that she'd object to that, but she didn't want things to become awkward or Thomas to feel pressured. Not when their friendship was growing. "We can see if he will. I guess it depends how busy he is with his job."

To Emma's relief her aunt didn't mention Thomas again during the conversation, but instead tossed out a few ideas she had for the festival. The excitement in the older woman's voice made Emma smile. This project would be good for Aunt Ginny. And if Thomas was able to help them with the festival, then that would be good for Emma.

~ ~ ~

The weekend had flown by, and before he knew it, Thomas was driving back towards the Florida panhandle. It had been a good weekend overall, especially since he'd accomplished some minor home repair tasks for his mother. He always tried to make sure and take care of house repairs and yard work while he was home, even though his mom did her best to be independent.

In his opinion, the only downside to the weekend was a talk with Avril about her ex-boyfriend coming back into her life. She admitted that Devin had been phoning her fairly often and wanted to come for a visit. Thomas had to choose his words so as not to upset his sister. But each time he thought about the young man fleeing the relationship he and Avril had shared, it sent his blood pressure rising.

His cell phone rang, snapping his mind back to the present. Even though he preferred not to talk while driving, he was on a straight stretch of road and traffic was light, so he decided a brief conversation would be okay, especially when he heard his buddy, Paul's voice coming through.

"Hey Thomas, are you back at your bungalow yet?"

"Hi, Paul. Nope, I've still got about forty-five minutes to go, I figure. How was your weekend?"

"Pretty good. Sorry I didn't get to stop by your Mom's house to see you and visit with Avril, but we had a family reunion so that's where this weekend went." Paul laughed, then asked a question that surprised Thomas. "So, any updates on the lady?"

"What lady?" Thomas couldn't resist playing dumb with his friend. He knew Paul meant well, and it was no secret that he wanted Thomas to find the right girl and settle down.

"You know who I'm referring to. Don't let her get away, man. You'll regret it. The clock is ticking and none of us are getting any younger. And don't forget, I've already volunteered to be the best man at your wedding, so that part is taken care of." Paul burst out laughing and Thomas couldn't suppress a grin.

"Thanks, buddy. I appreciate you looking out for me. And I promise you if and when anything develops, I'll let you know right away." The two friends visited a few more minutes before the call ended.

Thomas held the steering wheel with one hand and rubbed the back of his neck with the other. He hadn't realized until now how tired he was. Cleaning out the gutters at his mom's house this weekend had been more physically demanding than he'd thought at the time. But at least he got that chore accomplished for her.

Now he replayed his friend's words in his mind. Good ol' Paul—he really was looking out for Thomas. And he appreciated it. Yet his top priority was protecting his sister. How could he do that if he had a wife? Unless he had a wife who was compassionate and understood his feelings of protectiveness over Avril. Not many women would have those kinds of qualities. *Except maybe Emma.*

The thought entered his mind without bidding, and he knew that from everything he'd seen of Emma Hopkins, she was compassionate and kind. Not to mention his feelings grew stronger each time he was with her. But did she feel the same about him? He still wasn't sure exactly how she felt about him, and there was only one way to find out. He needed to see her more and let her know his feelings. After all, as his buddy had reminded him, the clock was ticking, and he wasn't getting any younger.

~ ~ ~

After agreeing to help Aunt Ginny with the church's summer festival, Emma hoped she was doing the right thing. Yet how could she refuse her sweet aunt? There was no way—she simply couldn't. So, she'd do her best and try to keep her social butterfly aunt from becoming too tired and overwhelmed with the responsibilities.

How interesting that Ginny had suggested asking Thomas to help. She may as well do that soon, because knowing her aunt, she'd keep asking until she learned if he could help. Hopefully she'd see him this week and would ask him then.

To her relief, she didn't have to wait long. That afternoon Thomas stopped by the gift shop before closing time, as he'd done in the past. Looking attractive in a pale, coral-colored shirt, he smelled wonderful too as his woodsy scent drifted to Emma's nose.

"Hi. How was your weekend?" She smiled up at him as he approached the counter where she was straightening a small display of inspirational bookmarks.

He grinned at her, his dark eyes dancing with delight. Was he glad to see her? She hoped so, but she mustn't get carried away. For all she knew, he'd just secured a sizable business account or something similar.

"My weekend was good, thanks for asking. Except I've been a bit sore today, as much as I hate admitting it." He chuckled as he explained. "I cleaned out the gutters for my mom since the weather was so nice. I also trimmed a few bushes in her yard, so I guess that physical exertion was a bit much for me, since most of my work is done behind a computer screen or in my car." He shook his head. "How about you? Did you have a nice weekend?" He sounded genuinely interested, another reminder of how different he was from her ex.

She gave a grinning nod. "Yes, thanks. It was pleasant, and we had a good-sized crowd at church yesterday." She hesitated and decided there was no time like the present. "Um…speaking of church, I have a question to ask. Actually, it's a favor my aunt wants me to ask you." Before Emma could say more, he rolled his eyes, making her giggle.

"Oh no…your Aunt Ginny doesn't want me to preach a sermon, does she? That's not my area of expertise." His features lit up with playful amusement that made her pulse race.

"No worries. I think we all agree that Pastor Jack does an excellent job with the sermons, not that you wouldn't deliver a good message yourself."

"Thanks for your vote of confidence, but I guess it's just as well the Lord hasn't called me into the ministry. I admire men like Pastor Jack who deliver a sermon without reading notes or stammering around. I'm sure my mind would go blank in the middle of my message." He shook his head, then smiled. "Now what was the favor your aunt needed?"

"Aunt Ginny is the epitome of outgoing and energetic, and she's volunteered to head up the church's first summer festival. Some of the church members talked about having one in the past, but no one ever took the initiative. This year Aunt Ginny offered, and she's counting on me to assist her, which I gladly will. But then she mentioned needing a few men to help with some of the physical work—you know, setting up tables and maybe even constructing some simple wooden games. And Ginny wondered if you'd be willing to help a little." Emma paused, trying to gauge his reaction. She didn't want him to regret visiting their church, and she also didn't want to put him on the spot if he would rather not help. She added. "Look, I know you've recently taken on more work in your job, so I'll understand if you can't commit to helping at all. I'm sure Ginny will understand too." To her relief he nodded.

"Sure, no problem. Just tell your aunt to let me know what I need to do, or, you can let me know. And I'll do my best to make sure I'm not on the road. I'll need to know the date of the festival and later on get an idea of what will be involved. But I'm happy to help out." His warm smile melted her heart. Was he for real? Surely all his kindness and wonderful qualities were not a façade, were they?

At that moment footsteps sounded from the

rear of the shop as Ginny hurried toward them. She was smiling, then glanced around the store. "No customers? Well, I guess we can go ahead and turn the sign to CLOSED."

Emma stepped to the door and flipped over the sign, relieved there were no customers so she and her aunt could give Thomas their full attention. As she returned to his side, she made sure to leave a gap between them. Even so, she felt a tingle that she hoped her aunt didn't notice.

Ginny spoke to Thomas, then sent a questioning glance to her niece.

Emma grinned and nodded. "Yes, I've asked Thomas about assisting with the summer festival, and he very kindly agreed."

Her aunt reached out and patted his arm. "Oh, bless your heart. Thank you so much, young man. And don't worry—it won't be overly-strenuous work. Just some lifting and possibly hammering now and then." She beamed up at him, obviously pleased. "You two young folks go ahead and visit a bit. I need to finish up a few things in the supply room." Her smile lingered on her niece, as if encouraging her to make the most of her time with Thomas. It was no secret her aunt wanted to see Emma in a romantic relationship.

Ginny said good-bye to Thomas before scurrying to the rear of the shop.

Emma didn't have a chance to say anything because Thomas grinned down at her. "I don't want to keep you here too long since it's closing time, and I'm sure you have things to do. But I wondered if you'd like to go to dinner on Thursday? Since I'm going home to Alabama again this weekend, I won't be in Coastal Breeze; otherwise I'd see if you wanted to do something then."

"Sure, that sounds good." Emma couldn't deny a twinge of disappointment that he was returning to his home yet again. Maybe he did have a female friend there he was seeing and was afraid to mention it to Emma. After all, that would be awkward and a little strange. As he eyed her, she shoved away the negative thoughts.

"Are you sure? If you already have other plans it's fine."

She chuckled while chiding herself for allowing her thoughts to stray. "Yes, I'm sure. That sounds nice, and wherever you'd like to eat is fine with me. I'd offer to cook for you, but after working here in the gift shop all day, I'm doing well to heat up a can of soup or microwave a meal." Instantly she regretted her words. Now he might think she couldn't cook or was lazy. Well, at least he knew she could bake cookies and he'd enjoyed those. But his next comments took away her worries.

"I understand. I'd never expect you to cook after being here working all day. Especially when you have a lot of customers. Dealing with the public—even when they're courteous—can be tiring." He laughed, then suggested the time to pick her up.

A few minutes later he exited the gift shop and Emma hurried to finish her tasks. When her aunt came out of the supply room and asked about her visit with Thomas, Emma knew it was her aunt's not-so-subtle way of finding out if Emma had a date lined up.

"Thomas asked me to eat out this Thursday. But if you need me to work later let me know."

Ginny shook her head. "My stars, Emma Jean. You go out and eat with that handsome young man. Work in the shop can be done when you and I are here." Her eyes twinkled.

In her cottage that evening, Emma's thoughts whirled with ideas for the summer festival and ways she could help her aunt. Then her thoughts switched gears to Thomas. If only she could enjoy being with him and not worry that he was hiding something. He'd already shown her that he was nothing like BG—not even close.

A silent reminder whispered to her at that moment. *Pray.* Then a wave of guilt washed over her. She knew that she'd not been praying nearly enough about this situation. As a Christian, Emma was certain that God did not want her spending the rest of her life living in fear. She must find a way to overcome her fear and reluctance to get involved because of what she'd gone through in the past.

~ ~ ~

Thomas still wasn't sure of Emma's feelings. At times she seemed to care about him, yet at other times she appeared distant, as she'd been after he'd asked her out to eat. There was still much about her he didn't know. Something in her past must have caused her to be extra-cautious.

Pushing those thoughts from his mind, he focused on the restaurant he was taking her to this evening, hoping his client's recommendation would be accurate. He pulled his car to a stop in front of

Emma's cottage as she was stepping out of her front door. His pulse raced at the thought of spending an evening with her.

As he helped her into his sports coupe, he caught a whiff of her fresh, citrusy cologne. She wore a teal-colored outfit that accentuated her chestnut hair, which hung loosely over her shoulders.

"I hope the restaurant we're going to will be good. A client insisted I try it, and he couldn't say enough wonderful things about it. Its specialty is seafood but he said there are other choices on the menu too."

"Sounds wonderful. I've been looking forward to this. I've worn off the peanut butter and jelly sandwich I had for lunch." She giggled, the sound pleasing to his ears. What was it about her that was so appealing to him? Everything. Yes, it was true. Her beauty, of course. But even more important were her gentle mannerisms, kind spirit, and her faith. If only Thomas could be sure that she cared for him.

After ordering their meals, the couple sat in a booth sipping iced tea and chatting about the restaurant's décor. "I like how they've draped fishnet around with the seashells in it. And all the paintings of lighthouses are lovely."

Thomas liked the way her eyes sparkled as she took in the sights around her. "Yes, this place isn't fancy, but it's nice, so I hope the food will be as good as my client said." He caught sight of another lighthouse painting he'd not noticed. "Wow, Avril would love that painting. When she visits Coastal

Breeze, I might need to bring her here." An idea suddenly formed.

"When my sister comes for a visit, I'd like you to meet her. And if it works with your schedule, you could go out to eat with us. Even though she's in a wheelchair, it's not a big deal. I always make sure the places we visit are handicapped accessible." He saw something in Emma's eyes. Was it pity? He glanced down at the placemat in front of him, then grabbed his glass of tea. No way could he tell her that he was the reason his sister was in a wheelchair.

Emma spoke softly and reached out to pat his hand. "I'd love to meet your sister. From what you've told me, it sounds like you're a wonderful brother to her." Her smile was sweet, and it was all he could do to keep from pouring out the whole story from three years ago.

The server appeared with their meals, so the conversation switched to the food. Both had platters of shrimp, crab cakes, hushpuppies, and a baked potato.

"It looks and smells wonderful, so I'm sure it tastes wonderful too." Emma grinned before bowing her head for a blessing.

Thomas offered up a brief prayer of thanks for their food, then smiled at her and spoke in a teasing tone. "Bon appétit." He winked at her. "You can tell I'm not French. That's all I know in that language." He was glad to see her giggling.

The remainder of their evening together was wonderful, and Thomas was struck yet again with how much he cared about her. Should he take a risk? He'd never know if their relationship stood a chance to grow unless he pressed on, so as he walked her to the door of her cottage, he took her hand in his. "I really had a nice time, Emma. Thank you for joining me. As I said before, if I wasn't going home this weekend I would've asked you out—if you didn't already have plans." He was rambling and about to make a fool of himself. When they reached her doorstep, she gazed up at him with eyes that he could melt in, and before he gave it another thought, he planted a gentle kiss on her lips. To his relief she didn't pull away.

As much as he wanted the kiss to linger, he didn't want to come on too strong or frighten her, so he pulled away and smiled. Her smile told him that she hadn't minded the kiss. And maybe, she even enjoyed it. He could only hope.

7

No way could she go to sleep. Not yet. Never mind that tomorrow would be Friday, and most likely a busy day in the gift shop. Yet Emma was so keyed up—in a good way—that she was certain sleep would not come for a while. She read her Bible, drank a glass of milk, read a chapter of the Christian novel she'd recently started, and then as a last resort, she turned on her television to the weather station. Nope, nothing was making her drowsy, and if sleep didn't take over, she'd be in a major fog at work tomorrow.

All she could think about was the brief but oh-so-sweet kiss that Thomas had given her. It had been totally unexpected but totally wonderful. Afterward, any awkward moments vanished. He'd told her he enjoyed their time together, then had added that he'd phone her from Alabama.

He couldn't be seeing another woman in

Alabama, could he? Deep down Emma really didn't think he was, yet that niggle of doubt continued to plague her. Well, she'd have to fight that doubt and keep praying.

It wasn't until midnight that she drifted into slumber and awoke feeling surprisingly well. *Must be that kiss.* The thought made her giggle. She knew she'd better be careful around Ginny or her well-meaning aunt would leap ahead and start planning for wedding bells.

"Hello there, dear one." Ginny glanced up from some inventory paperwork when Emma entered the shop at eight o'clock. "How was your dinner with Thomas last evening?" Even though the older woman appeared to be looking over her notes, Emma knew it was a guise. She knew without a doubt that her aunt was about to burst to know details. There was no doubt her aunt adored Thomas.

"It was great. That meal was one of the best I've ever had. You need to eat there if you haven't. You'd especially like the shrimp." Emma pretended to be focused on sorting through a box of books to be shelved, but she could feel her aunt's eyes on her.

"I've heard it's delicious, so I'll have to see if one of my widowed friends might like to join me there sometime soon." She paused and cleared her throat. "Did you and Thomas talk a lot? I sure hope he won't continue traveling home to Alabama each weekend, and that'll give you two more time together."

Emma could feel the blush creeping up her

face. No way was she mentioning the good-night kiss to her aunt. No way.

"Yes, we visited a good bit. But I'm not sure about his weekend schedule. He likes to go home to check on his handicapped sister and to help his mom, which is really nice of him. From what he's said, he does a lot of yard work and household repairs for his mom, since his dad has passed away."

Ginny nodded and smiled. "Yes, Thomas certainly is a nice young man. The fact that he's so caring about his sister and mother is a very good sign." She didn't say any more at the moment, but Emma could read her aunt's thoughts. Ginny may as well have told her to be careful and not let him get away.

The weekend flew by, and although her thoughts returned to Thomas often, she kept busy with her chores, errands, and work on the summer festival plans. Her aunt had given her suggestions that the other committee members had offered, so Emma combined those with a few ideas of her own and compiled a master plan for the event. She had to admit she was already enjoying this more than she'd thought she would.

On Sunday evening Thomas called her, and although Emma was thrilled to hear from him, she tried to keep a level tone and not sound too eager. "How was your weekend?"

He laughed. "Busy. Very busy. I did more yard work for Mom and took her and my sister shopping at some new stores that have opened up in our small town. But it was good spending time with them.

They've both told me they look forward to my weekend visits." He chuckled before asking about her weekend.

Trying to sound upbeat as she mentioned plans for the festival, Emma's heart sunk. If his mother and sister looked forward to his weekend visits that much, then Thomas would likely continue heading to Alabama each Friday. After all, he was such a caring guy and obviously very committed to his family. Which was a good thing. Except when he was in Alabama he was far away from Coastal Breeze and Emma.

You're being selfish. Stop thinking about yourself, and think about Thomas's widowed mother and his sister in a wheelchair. The silent chiding caused guilt to wash over her, so she ignored her earlier thoughts and continued talking about the summer festival.

"Remember if you have any ideas or suggestions for the festival, please let us know. Aunt Ginny is open to more ideas, and I am too. Besides, she's already confessed to me that she's fearful if this first festival flops, the church members will not want to consider having another one in the future."

"Well then, we'll have to do everything we can to make it a success." Emma could tell he was sincere, and it sent a warmth rushing through her.

"Would you and your aunt like to have dinner with me one evening this week? I thought then maybe the three of us could talk about the festival."

"That sounds great. I'll mention it to her when we open the gift shop in the morning. Is there a particular day that would work for you? As far as I know, Ginny doesn't have anything extra going on this week besides running the shop and working on anything festival-related."

"How about Thursday? Unless that doesn't work for you or your aunt."

"Sounds good. As I said I'll check with Ginny first thing tomorrow, but Thursday should work. I'll go ahead and let you know my aunt will want to pay for our meals. So be prepared." Emma giggled, yet underneath she felt a bit of disappointment. Since Thomas hadn't suggested eating out on Friday, that likely meant he was planning to return to Alabama. His family came first, and they needed him. If she wanted to continue seeing him, she'd have to accept the fact that his life was already full.

~ ~ ~

Two weeks later the festival plans were in full swing. Thomas had explained to his mother and sister that he wouldn't be coming home every weekend, and to his surprise, Avril seemed fine with that. Of course, his mom was glad he was finding a life in Coastal Breeze, especially since she'd been encouraging him to develop friends and possibly a romantic relationship. He had a strong feeling his mom and sister would love Emma if they had the opportunity to meet her.

"You are so kind to help us with the festival." The elderly lady named Midge smiled up at him, her bright pink lipstick a tiny bit smeared at the corners of her mouth. Even though Thomas tried not to judge, he'd pegged this sweet lady right away as the church busybody. Midge enjoyed keeping up with everyone else's life and happenings.

He gave her a polite smile and nodded. "I'm happy to help out. I enjoy feeling like I'm part of a church again, especially since my home church is in Alabama." He noticed the older woman stepped a few inches closer, and he wondered if she was about to whisper something to him.

Midge cast a quick glance around before speaking in a lowered voice. "I think it's wonderful you've been so attentive to Ginny's sweet niece. Emma is a beautiful young lady and she deserves someone nice like you." She hesitated only a few seconds before plunging ahead with information that shocked Thomas. "From what I've heard, the man she dated before was a real thug. Involved in drugs and who knows what else. Then he turned up dead! There were rumors he might've been murdered. Isn't that terrible? Poor Emma—knowing she'd been seeing someone like that. And now she worries that one of his thug friends might be after her." Clasping her arms tightly around her chest, Midge paused and shook her head. "Just terrible. That poor girl deserves much better, so as I've said, I'm thankful you're in the picture now." She put her hand up to her mouth in a whispering gesture. "And so is Ginny. But you don't need to tell Ginny or Emma I said this." Midge giggled like a young girl before hobbling toward a table that held a coffee pot, soft drinks, and snacks.

Thomas was more than a little dumbfounded. He watched Midge pour herself a cup of coffee. At the moment he felt like pouring a bottle of cold water over his head. Had he heard Midge's words correctly?

Yet he knew he had. How could Emma ever be involved with someone of such unsavory character? Midge had used the term *thug* and had mentioned drugs. That was totally out-of-character for the sweet, gentle Emma Hopkins that he knew. *Maybe you don't know her as well as you thought.* Could she have a hidden side that she'd kept concealed from him? Or maybe she used to be wild and had since settled down. He knew people could change. But it was hard to imagine Emma ever being involved with a guy who fit the description Midge had shared with him. Not only that, but the thought that someone might be after Emma sent his heart racing.

Thomas gazed across the church grounds at Emma. She was all smiles as she talked with her aunt and several other ladies who were on the festival committee. It was obvious she was enjoying herself, and he had no doubts this upcoming festival would be a success.

It was as if she knew he was watching her, because her gaze shifted to his, then she waved. He forced a smile and waved in return. He must be careful to not let her know what Midge had shared. Emma would be horrified if she knew he knew about her past.

A voice from within interrupted his thoughts. *What about your own past? What would Emma think if she knew you'd been the cause of your sister's horrible accident? All because you sent her a text while she was driving, and she replied to it.*

This was not accomplishing anything. He'd

come here today to help with the church festival, so that was what he needed to do. He strode toward Emma and the group of ladies. As he approached them, Aunt Ginny gushed.

"Ladies, has everyone met Thomas? He's Emma's friend and has kindly agreed to help us with any physical labor. You know—like lifting heavy items and hammering." She beamed proudly and glanced around the small cluster of elderly females. They all eyed him, making him feel he was on display.

Thomas nodded and smiled at each lady. "I'm happy to lend a hand. The one time I visited your church everyone was welcoming, so I don't mind helping at all." He felt Emma's eyes on him, and was relieved when all the other ladies scurried away to attend to their tasks. Only he and Emma remained, and she smiled up at him, the mid-day sun making her green eyes sparkle.

"I hope you're not regretting your decision to help us." She tucked a wayward strand of hair behind one ear.

He shook his head. "No, not a bit. As I told those ladies, I'm happy to help. Now what should I be doing?" He glanced around to see if any building supplies had been delivered because he preferred to construct signs or a cornhole game to standing around.

Emma peered at the list she held in her hands, then smiled up at him. "If you don't mind, you could go ahead and work on the fishing game. Mr. Weaver is also going to be helping—have you met him?" She gestured toward an older man in work clothes and a ballcap.

"No, I don't believe I have."

Emma led Thomas over to Mr. Weaver, and after brief introductions and explanations about the fishing game, the two men got to work as Emma walked toward her aunt. Moments later, Thomas overheard the ladies laughing as they discussed the best area for the baked goods table.

Thomas and Mr. Weaver kept their conversation to a minimum, which was fine with him. He was still absorbing the information the well-meaning Midge had shared with him, and he wasn't sure how to handle it. Lost in his private thoughts, Thomas wasn't paying enough attention to the saw in his right hand, and the steel blade sliced into the edge of his left hand. Searing pain ripped through his hand. Blood gushed from the cut. After a loud gasp Mr. Weaver was at his side, calling for his wife to come and assist.

Don't faint. You cannot faint. Thomas forced himself to stop looking at his injured hand now saturated with crimson blood. Thankfully Mrs. Weaver had pulled over a folding chair and insisted he sit. Pain coursed through his left hand. Embarrassment washed over when Emma joined the others hovering over him.

"What do you need me to do?" Emma directed her question to the no-nonsense woman who was wiping off his hand and applying pressure.

"If you would step inside the building and look in the church office. There should be a first-aid kit in the small closet on your left."

"I'll get it right away." Emma dashed off,

making Thomas feel even more ridiculous. Ladies hovering over him and helping—all from a gash he got because he wasn't focused on what he was doing.

Ginny patted his other arm, offering a soothing reminder that he'd be fine.

Thomas cringed at her words. "I feel so foolish. I should've been watching more closely as I used that saw. I'm not much help today, am I?"

To his surprise, Mrs. Weaver grinned at him. "Oh, don't fret about this. Why, my husband injures himself on a regular basis, it seems. Each spring I tell him we need to hire someone to do our yard work and house repairs, but he insists that he's the man of the house and can take care of everything." She laughed, making Thomas feel better.

"I guess that's the way a lot of men are, myself included. We think we can handle it all, but we usually can't." He noticed Emma sprinting toward him with the first-aid kit.

Later his hand was bandaged, and Mrs. Weaver had assured him she didn't think stitches were necessary. "Had you cut deeper, then we'd be taking you to the emergency room. But this bandage should take care of it. Just be careful with that hand and don't let the area become infected." She put away the medical supplies.

"I can't thank you enough. I apologize that I did something so dumb and haven't contributed anything toward the festival work today." With downcast eyes, Thomas glanced at Emma and the Weavers.

They all smiled at him as Ginny commented.

"No, you added some excitement to the day. Look at it this way. Now everyone will be more careful—especially when using sharp tools. So you gave us our safety lesson." She winked at him and Emma giggled.

Mr. Weaver stepped closer and patted his shoulder. "Don't worry, son. There will be plenty for you to do later on, I'm sure. You take care of that hand and I'll finish up this fishing game."

Thomas thanked him and Mrs. Weaver, then moved closer to Emma. Gesturing toward his bandaged hand, he shrugged. "Sorry this happened. I really wanted to help with the festival work today."

She looked up at him, unmistakable tenderness showing in her gaze. "No worries, I'm just sorry you were hurt. We've still got plenty of time before the festival, so I'm certain everything will be ready. Why don't you sit over here and I'll get you a drink. "She led the way to several chairs not far from the snack table.

Thomas followed along, the information from Midge still hovering in his thoughts.

Minutes later, they sat together sipping on cold soft drinks. She was doing her best to help him feel less embarrassed, he knew.

"I got tickled by what Mrs. Weaver shared about her husband always getting hurt. Poor Mr. Weaver." She stirred the ice and took another sip of her drink, then continued. "I'm glad your injury wasn't worse. I used to know someone who worked on a construction job, and he got in the way of a nail gun one time." She cringed and shook her head.

Without intending to, Thomas blurted out words he instantly regretted. "Was that the thug you knew who was involved with drugs?" Immediately he wished he could take back his question—especially when he saw Emma's face.

She looked at him with a mixture of confusion and hurt. "What did you say?" Then she shook her head. "Never mind." She turned away from him and peered off into the distance.

"Oh Emma, I'm so sorry. I should never have said that. It's just that earlier today Midge was talking with me, and she volunteered some information about a guy you'd dated. She said he was a thug and into drugs. It sounded bad, and I couldn't imagine you being with a person like that." Was he making it worse?

The defiance on her face was hard to miss. "I'm surprised Midge shared that with you. How on earth did that even come up in your conversation?" She angrily took a swig of her drink, then plopped the cup on the ground beside her feet.

Thomas attempted to explain that Midge had been complimenting him, but then mentioned the guy from Emma's past. "I think she had good intentions and was trying to look out for you." He tried to ignore the throbbing in his injured hand and focus on saying the right words to this troubled woman seated next to him, who most likely would scurry away at any minute. And could he blame her?

He cleared his throat and continued. "I got the impression that because she's friends with your aunt, Midge wants to make certain you're happy.

Anyway, I guess when she shared that information with me, it took me by surprise. I'm sorry I said anything." How he hoped his words soothed her feelings. If only he could take back what he'd spoken a few minutes ago. But that was impossible.

Emma lifted her chin and looked directly into his eyes. With pursed lips, she spoke, her words clipped. "Midge may have had good intentions, but she shouldn't have been so quick to share my personal information." She reached up and swiped at loose hairs over her eyes. "But I know she's elderly and wants to be a mother hen, still making sure everyone is taken care of." She shrugged, then stood. "I'm glad your hand didn't require stitches. But since you've hurt it, there's no need for you to try and do any work here today. I think everyone else can manage if you want to head home." She offered a forced smile, then picked up her cup and walked away.

Thomas sat for a few moments longer, watching her walk toward a group of ladies who were peering over some notes. He blew out a sigh, and using his good hand, picked up his cup and headed toward the trash bag. Emma was right—he may as well return home. He could, at least, finish some work for his job and watch a movie. Yet as he walked toward his parked car, his heart was heavy, and he had an ominous feeling he'd blown it with Emma.

~ ~ ~

"You're extra energetic this afternoon, Emma dear. By the way, did Thomas leave? I imagine his hand must've been hurting badly after that nasty cut from the saw." Ginny glanced around the work area before looking at her niece.

"Yes. I told him he might as well return home since he didn't need to work with an injured hand." She remained silent about the reason for her energy level at the moment. The more she thought about Midge sharing her personal information with Thomas, not to mention the comment he'd made to her, the madder she felt. Yet, in all honesty, she didn't harbor anger toward the older woman. Midge was Midge. Anyone who knew her understood that was part of her personality, though some aptly labeled her a busybody. But Thomas had no right to make that judgmental comment about being surprised she would associate with someone like her ex-boyfriend. He knew nothing about what she'd gone through.

"Okay, these prizes are all sorted, and I've got a schedule made out for the fish pond workers and the jellybean jars." She reached up and rubbed her shoulders, aware of the stiffness in her muscles.

Mrs. Weaver approached Emma and Ginny. "Jellybean jars? What are those?" Her serious expression softened into an amused look of curiosity.

Emma laughed and explained. "It's a jar filled with candy, such as jellybeans, and the child tries to guess the number of pieces inside the jar. The child with the closest guess wins a prize. I have to admit I'm terrible at guessing games like that, but it's fun to watch the children. And I like seeing them eyeing all that candy in each jar." Emma giggled and sent herself a mental reminder to buy more jellybeans for the candy dish in her cottage.

"That does sound fun. But I'm afraid I wouldn't be good at guessing the amount either." Mrs. Weaver's eyes scanned the room. "I'm assuming your friend went home? I'm glad he didn't require stitches for that cut."

Trying to keep her tone casual, Emma nodded. "Yes, ma'am. I'm glad too. And I told him earlier to head home instead of trying to work here with one hand." After a brief pause, she offered a smile to the middle-aged nurse. "Thank you again for your help, Mrs. Weaver. I'm not sure what we would've done if you hadn't been here to put your nursing skills to work."

Aunt Ginny nodded in agreement. "Oh my, yes! Emma is right. We appreciate you so much, Wilma." Mrs. Weaver blushed at the praise, unable to hide her pleasure at the compliments.

"It wasn't much effort at all. And I'm always happy to help if anyone is sick or hurt." The nurse replied and shrugged. "I'd better head home with Walter. I think he's reached his limit doing handyman chores today." She chuckled.

The more people she met in Coastal Breeze, the more Emma felt she belonged here, regardless of whether Thomas remained in the town or not. Besides, after his earlier comment, she might be better off not having a relationship with him. Even a very casual one. So why did that thought make her feel sad?

~ ~ ~

"Yeah, I went to do some work and instead ended up hurting my hand. It was really a dumb thing to do." Thomas held the phone with his right hand, trying to ignore the pain in his left one as he talked with Paul. "I guess I'm more cut out to work behind a computer." Knock on wood that he wouldn't hurt himself doing chores for his mother.

"Don't be hard on yourself, buddy. It happens to the best of us. At least you weren't painting and ended up pouring paint on yourself. Talk about a mess. And an embarrassment." Paul laughed as he recounted a funny story from his past, giving Thomas a much-needed lift.

Thirty minutes later the call ended and Thomas heated up a microwave meal for his supper. If he hadn't hurt himself and then upset Emma, he might be driving the two of them to a nice seafood restaurant right now. He released a sigh. Oh well. His hand would heal and return to normal, but was his relationship with Emma beyond help? Had he done too much damage with his words?

As he ate his meatloaf dinner and tried not to think of how he could've been enjoying a shrimp platter with an ocean view, Thomas replayed Midge's words in his mind. *A thug. Involved in drugs. Turned up dead.* It was still hard to wrap his mind around the fact that Emma would associate with someone like that—much less date the guy.

Even though he wanted their relationship to continue, Thomas knew he'd have to learn the truth about what happened in Emma's past. If the questions he had remained unanswered, they would fester, and he'd never feel he could completely be at ease with her. Yet for all he knew, Emma didn't want to continue their relationship. The seething looks she'd given him before he left the church hovered in his mind like a dark cloud.

No, he cared too much about her. So somehow or another, he would have to make things right with her again. But he would also have to learn the truth about her past. Now he wondered if she'd be willing to open up and share details about her past, and if not, then there was nothing else he could do.

After a fitful night of sleep, he decided to stay home and view a church service on his television. Not that anyone would miss him at the Coastal Breeze church—after all, he was technically a visitor there. Maybe later he'd take a walk on the beach for some fresh air. He was thankful his upcoming week would be busy, and then he'd return to Alabama on Friday for the weekend. He knew the busier he stayed, the less time he had to dwell on thoughts of what had happened with Emma.

At one o'clock someone knocked at the door of his bungalow, startling him from gazing at figures on his computer screen. As he hurried toward the door, he could tell a woman stood outside. Aunt Ginny, alone and clutching a casserole dish.

"Aunt Ginny. This is a surprise. Would you like to come in?" He gestured with his injured hand and smiled at her.

"Hello there, how's your hand today?" She edged a bit closer to his doorway.

"A little better, thank you for asking. Are you sure you won't come inside?"

"Only to set down this dish I prepared for you. It's a beef and noodle casserole that I hope you'll enjoy. There's enough that it should last you for at least two or three meals. It reheats well in the microwave." She smiled up at him, then headed back toward the door to leave.

From the aroma drifting up from the covered rectangular dish, Thomas was certain it would taste delicious. The sandwich he'd eaten earlier hadn't been very filling.

"Thank you so much. This is very kind of you, but I hope you didn't go to trouble for me. I'm fine, really." He was embarrassed standing here talking with Emma's aunt. Did Ginny know what had transpired between the couple the previous day? Might as well venture a question and see. "How is Emma?"

A curious look flitted across her face and she offered a guarded smile. "She's okay. I'm afraid she's been working too hard, though. I'm trying to encourage her to slow down and enjoy living at the coast." Her eyes lingered on his face a moment longer, causing Thomas to wonder if Ginny was going to say more about her niece. She didn't.

"Enjoy the casserole, and take care of that injured hand. And by the way, no rush on getting the dish back to me. I've got several casserole dishes, so you take your time with that one." She grinned at him before turning to head out.

He called out his thanks again, then gently closed the door. Ginny's perfume lingered in the air of his bungalow, and he smiled. He could imagine his mother and Aunt Ginny getting along well. Kind of like a couple of mothers-in-law? The unexpected question teased his mind and he shoved it away. No, he wasn't even close to such a relationship with Emma that would enable her aunt and his mother to see each other on a regular basis. Right now, he needed to see where he stood with Emma, and learn what she was hiding.

PATTI JO MOORE

8

"That was such a nice thing for you to do, Aunt Ginny." Emma smiled at her aunt before returning her focus to preparing the gift shop to open the next morning.

"Well, Thomas has no family here, and he had good intentions to help us with the summer festival. So when he injured his hand and was stuck in his bungalow, I thought he might enjoy a home-cooked meal." Ginny laughed and shook her head. "Of course, I just took a casserole. Next time I need to add some bread, side dishes, and dessert." She appeared to be pondering her words and making plans for another meal.

Next time? How often was her kind aunt planning on visiting Thomas? There was no doubt Ginny was fond of him and would be thrilled to see her niece in a long-term relationship with him. But after what had happened, Emma didn't see much of a relationship now. And to her dismay, the thought made her sad, but she must guard her heart, because no way was she setting herself up to be hurt again. Memories of BG tried to force their way into her mind, but she shoved them away. Instead, she focused on a summer-themed display.

"You're doing a nice job with the displays. Must be that creative eye you have. Speaking of which, how's your photography coming along? You'd mentioned a while back that you wanted to do a lot of ocean-related photos." Ginny appeared genuinely interested, so Emma told her about several recent shots she'd captured on the beach.

Ginny's eyes widened, and she tapped her bottom lip with a finger. "You know, dear, if you'd like you could frame some of your photos and sell them here in the shop." She stepped closer, as if eager to see her niece's reaction.

Even though Emma was always comfortable around her beloved aunt, she could feel a heated blush rising on her face. She put a hand up to her mouth. "Oh, that is so kind of you to offer. But I'm certainly not a professional—in fact, far from it. My photography is just a hobby I enjoy. I doubt anyone would be interested in purchasing my pictures."

"It might be a hobby and you may not be a professional, but I don't think you realize just how talented you are. Your photos are fantastic, and I think others would agree." Ginny smiled as if she couldn't be more certain her words were true.

Never wanting to be in the spotlight, even with her aunt, Emma thanked her, then turned her focus to the display, glad it was almost time for the shop to open for business.

Throughout the day Emma's thoughts kept returning to her aunt's early-morning comments about her photography. Maybe she should select some of her better beach-themed shots and frame them, then see if any would sell, or at least garner any interest. What did she have to lose? In fact, the more she thought about the idea, the more she decided that's what she would do.

Late that afternoon she was about to head to the beach for her usual pre-supper stroll, but this time decided to bring along her camera. Maybe she'd snap a few photos of the high tide waves or some seagulls swooping down for fish. She'd have to be careful of the lighting though. At this time of day the sun's rays were still so bright, and she didn't want any glare.

A few others sauntered along the shore, mostly tourists, although she was sure some of the local residents enjoyed walking this time of day as she did. With her camera strap around her neck, she walked along at a brisk pace, being watchful for a good photo opportunity.

As a cluster of gulls skittered along the water's edge, she lifted her camera and snapped two shots before the birds flew off. Then she captured a few more of the waves cresting as sunlight shimmered on the teal water. She hoped the pictures turned out. The breeze had picked up and she had a difficult time keeping her hair away from her face and eyes. This was enough for today.

"Emma!" The sudden voice calling her name startled her to the point that she almost dropped her camera, which would've proven disastrous. With a pounding heart and shaking hands, she whirled around on the wet sand.

Thomas sprinted toward her, his face not smiling but appearing apprehensive. She remained where she was, clutching her camera as if hanging on for dear life.

He stopped about two feet from her and offered a smile. "I hope I didn't startle you."

Emma reached up and brushed back some wayward strands of hair, knowing the increasing wind would only send them into her face again. She needed to return to her cottage. Besides, the sea spray wouldn't do her camera any good. Forcing a smile, she shrugged. "Yes, hearing my name when I'm in the middle of shooting pictures does catch me off-guard." She attempted a chuckle and hoped she didn't sound rude. She had not expected to see Thomas today.

"I'm sorry. I didn't think about that. But I wanted to catch you and was afraid you'd start walking on down the beach, and I need to hurry and get back to my bungalow. I'm expecting a call from my boss this evening about a new project we're working on. We don't normally have business calls so late in the day, but with his schedule, it worked out that way for today. Are you about to head back?" He gestured toward the starting point for their walks.

Emma nodded and put the cover back on her camera lens. It was a good thing she hadn't planned on more shots today. Besides, the sun was sinking fast now anyway, and she needed to return home and eat supper.

They walked along the shore for a few minutes with neither of them speaking. The waves crashing and a few seagulls squawking were the only sounds, and Emma was glad he couldn't hear her thumping heart. She assumed he must have a reason for catching up with her on the beach, especially since he was expecting a phone call from his boss.

Thomas stopped walking, turned, and gazed into her eyes as if searching for something. "Look, I wanted to apologize for what I said to you last weekend. That sounded judgmental of me, and I'm really sorry. Midge took me by surprise when she volunteered information about your past, and I guess it kind of stunned me. But I was wrong to say anything about that to you, and again I am sorry. Will you forgive me?"

She had not expected this, and certainly not today on the beach. And even though his words from last Saturday still bothered her a lot, Emma had to admit his apology came across as sincere. She peered up at him and nodded. "Yes, I forgive you. Although what you said did hurt because you assumed I have a questionable past, which I don't." She clamped her lips together, feeling emotional. The last thing she wanted to do was break down and cry in front of Thomas. She turned and continued toward the parking lot where she had begun her walk.

He reached out and patted her arm. "I know, and again I'm sorry. I had no right at all to say those things. But if you'll please forgive me and give me another chance, I will guard my mouth better." He cast a quick glance at her and grinned, reminding her of a little boy asking for a second chance.

When they reached the parking lot, Emma turned and faced him. "Yes, I do forgive you. Now you'd better go so you won't miss your boss's call, and I hope it goes well." She gave him her best smile, while clasping her camera.

"Okay, thanks. How about if I call you tomorrow and we can make plans to go out again?" The look of expectancy in his eyes turned her insides to mush, and all she could do was nod again and mumble an "okay."

After she finished her supper, as she got her clothes ready for the next day, the scene with Thomas on the beach replayed in her mind. Yes, his words last weekend had hurt her, but he'd apologized and seemed truly sincere. Still, she needed to guard her heart. But there was no doubt she was looking forward to his phone call about setting up another date.

~ ~ ~

He'd asked for forgiveness from Emma, so what else could he do? Thomas ran a hand down his tired face that night and tried to stay focused on the business call he'd just had with his boss about a new project. Exciting stuff, yet Thomas's mind didn't remain there after the call. Why was he so consumed with thoughts of Emma? *Because you've fallen in love with her. You just don't want to admit it.* The silent voice might as well have been a slap in his face as the truth registered with him.

The next morning, he gulped down coffee as he pored over his laptop. *Concentrate.* If he was going to be successful in his new position, he must do a good job with this latest project his boss had entrusted to him. Yet the image of a certain woman kept finding its way into his thoughts. At that moment he made up his mind that as soon as he finished the most urgent of his day's business, he'd phone Emma and plan a date.

Hours later, after he'd managed to accomplish a decent amount of work that day, he dialed Emma's number. She'd still be at the gift shop, but if she was busy, he'd leave a voice mail.

"Hello?" Emma's breathless voice answered on the third ring. Hearing her brought a smile to his face.

"Hi Emma. I'm sure you're still at work, so is this a busy time? If so, we can talk later."

"No, this is okay. There's only one customer in the shop right now and Aunt Ginny is helping her." Was she breathless from rushing or because she was glad that he was the caller?

His question was answered right away.

"Sorry I'm out of breath. I've been restocking some shelves, and when I heard my phone, I had to rush into the supply room to grab it." So much for him being the reason for her breathlessness.

Thomas chuckled. "It's fine. I was hesitant about phoning you while you're still working, but I wanted to go ahead and see if we could plan something. Maybe a dinner tomorrow evening?" He realized he was holding his breath while waiting for her response.

To his relief, she agreed, and in a matter of minutes, they planned to eat at their favorite seafood restaurant the next day. As soon as he clicked off his phone, Thomas had an idea. He'd buy her some flowers.

He pondered the most convenient place to purchase a small bouquet. With any luck, the flowers would help Emma forget his harsh words. Because the more he thought about her, the more he realized how much he wanted their relationship to grow.

~ ~ ~

"In my book, if a man brings flowers to a lady it means something special." Ginny's eyes twinkled as she pretended to focus on the jewelry display she'd been fiddling with for the past ten minutes.

Emma couldn't suppress a giggle. Her aunt was easy to read, and right now Ginny was tickled that her niece had received a bouquet from Thomas the previous evening.

"By the way, you are keeping enough water in the vase, aren't you?" Her aunt's gaze flitted to the lovely glass container on the counter behind the check-out area.

"Yes, ma'am. There's plenty of water, so hopefully they'll last a while." Emma allowed her eyes to linger on the colorful, fragrant blooms in the vase. Yellow roses, red carnations, and pink Stargazer lilies sent their perfume drifting lightly through the air. Emma didn't mention that she'd snapped several photos of the flowers the previous evening after Thomas brought her home from their date. When he'd arrived at her cottage door holding the vase of blooms, she'd been stunned but thrilled. Not wanting to leave them at home during the day, she'd decided to bring them to the gift shop so others could enjoy their beauty and fragrance.

What she hadn't planned on was having so many of the local customers asking questions about the flowers, and Emma had to smile as she thought about the grins and implied comments from several women who attended their church.

At the end of the day, she placed the flowers in her car to make the two-minute drive to her cottage. A sense of relief prevailed over her since she and Thomas were back on good terms, even though she still wanted to remain cautious. As if on cue, her cell rang as she pulled into her short driveway and turned off the engine.

"Hi Emma. Are you still at work?" Hearing his voice sent a tingle down her spine.

"No, I've just arrived home and am about to carry my vase of flowers into my cottage."

Thomas chuckled. "You took the flowers to work with you?"

"Yes, no sense leaving them in an empty house all day, and this way the customers could enjoy them too. Not to mention Aunt Ginny. She loved them." *And she's pretty fond of you, too.* Emma wasn't about to verbalize that thought, however.

"Well, that's good. I'd hoped you would enjoy them. I wanted to say hello and see if you'd be around this weekend because my sister Avril is coming for a brief visit. I'd like you to meet her."

Emma's heart gave a little leap. She'd looked forward to meeting his sister, but wasn't sure if he'd ever bring her to Coastal Breeze. "That's great. I look forward to meeting her."

"Sounds good. I'll drive to Alabama on Friday and return on Saturday with Avril. She'll only be here one night, but I figure that's long enough to show her around and then I'll drive her back to Alabama on Sunday."

"Thank you for letting me know, and I look forward to meeting her since I've heard so much about her." A sudden idea popped into Emma's mind. "Is there some kind of little gift I could give her? Just to make her feel welcome here?" She hoped Thomas wouldn't misunderstand her intentions. A small gift would not be because she felt sorry for the wheelchair-bound young woman, but rather to show kindness. To her relief, his response and tone sounded appreciative.

"That's really nice. Thank you for wanting to do that. If you'd like to get something small for her, that would be more than kind. She likes lighthouses, if that's any help." He chuckled.

"Okay, that's a big help, because that gives me several ideas of some items in the gift shop that I might purchase for her."

Since her car had become warm while she sat talking on the phone, Emma knew she'd better get her flowers inside and refill the water before they started to wilt. Once he ended their call, she scooted in, clasping the glass vase with both hands.

That evening she kept thinking about Avril. What would it be like meeting her in person? Thomas must be a wonderful big brother, and Emma was honored that he wanted his sister to meet her. She'd do whatever she could to make the young woman feel welcome. Hopefully, Avril would be pleased with the gifts Emma planned on giving her. And as much as she hated admitting it—even to herself—she also hoped Avril's brother would be pleased.

~ ~ ~

"You are very talented." Emma admired a small painting that Avril had done, as Thomas stood behind her wheelchair and beamed proudly.

"I told you my little sis has talent. She's amazing." He gently patted Avril's shoulder, and she ducked her head in obvious embarrassment.

It was Saturday afternoon and Emma had only met the younger woman an hour earlier. Thomas had picked up a pizza and insisted Emma join them at his bungalow for lunch, where he introduced his sister to her.

Emma had been a bit apprehensive at meeting her, as she hadn't been sure how physically limited Avril would be. She didn't want her to feel awkward or uncomfortable, but other than Thomas's raving praise of his sister, she seemed to be at ease.

Now the three adults were at the small kitchen table in the bungalow, visiting and talking about Coastal Breeze. Emma had been touched by how doting Thomas was to Avril, and also how easy it was to converse with her—especially since she and Emma had not met before that day.

"I told Little Sis if she can visit more often, there should be lots of good painting opportunities. Even though there are no lighthouses here." He winked at her.

"Oh, that reminds me." Emma excused herself

from the table, hurried to her bag, and carefully lifted out the small gifts she'd bought for Avril at the gift shop. "Here are a few little gifts to make you feel welcome here at the coast." Emma set the pink gift bag on the table in front of her.

Avril's eyes opened wide, and she blushed. "Presents for me?" She asked slowly, as if making sure she'd heard correctly. Her hands trembled slightly, and she nibbled her bottom lip.

"Yeah, I told you Emma's pretty nice, didn't I?" Now Thomas winked at her, causing her heart rate to increase. *What was it about this man?* She returned her focus to his sister. "It's just a few little items I hope you'll like."

As she slowly unwrapped the first gift, Avril's hazel eyes glowed, letting Emma know she was pleased. "How pretty! I love lighthouses. How did you know?" Her eyes darted from Emma to her brother and back again.

Emma grinned. "Okay, I had a little help. A certain someone told me that you love lighthouses." Thomas eyed her appreciatively, and a warmth ran through her.

Avril appeared to like the scented candle and the lightly-perfumed soap. With glistening eyes, she smiled up at Emma. "Thank you so much. You'd make a good sister." She reached out a hand and Emma extended hers for a gentle squeeze.

Emma couldn't think of a greater compliment than the one Avril had just given her. To lighten the mood, she shook her head. "You're sweet to say that. But my brother back in Georgia might not agree with you." They all laughed.

After visiting for another hour, Emma hugged Avril good-bye. Thomas escorted Emma to her car, then, in a soft voice, paid her a heartwarming compliment.

"Thanks for bringing those gifts and being so attentive to her. I don't think I've ever seen Avril take to someone as quickly as she took to you. At least…not since the accident." His eyes pooled with unshed tears, making Emma wonder yet again about the terrible accident that put his younger sister in a wheelchair.

"She's a sweetheart. I'm happy I could meet her and spend time visiting. Thanks again for the pizza. I'm so stuffed I probably won't eat supper." She laughed, relieved to see Thomas back to his normal self.

In her cottage that evening, Emma replayed her visit with Avril. Such a sweet young woman, but how sad she was confined to a wheelchair. Emma would add Avril to her prayer list. Thomas had mentioned a while back that his sister's physical therapy sessions had helped her immensely, and he clung to the hope she'd walk again someday.

A buzz from her phone interrupted her thoughts. Molly's text asked if Emma had time to talk. She called her friend's number, happy to hear Molly's voice. "Hey there, what's going on?"

"I thought I'd better give you a heads-up about BG's mother. She wants to meet with you again."

Emma drew in a deep, shuddering breath. "Why? Did she say?"

"No, just that she wanted to share something with you. I told her that you stay really busy in your new town, but that I'd pass along her message."

"Okay, I guess the next time I visit Dad I can see her then. I'd thought about driving home next weekend, and I was going to see if you'd be available for dinner and a girl talk while I'm home."

Molly squealed. "Absolutely! You'd better let me know when you're headed this way because I'd be upset if I found out later you'd been home and I didn't know about it." Both women laughed.

The friends chatted a while longer, and Molly said that she'd tell BG's mom that Emma would be in touch when she arrived back in Westville.

After the call ended, Emma's mind raced. She anticipated her trip home with a mixture of happiness and dread. She'd be thrilled to see her father and Molly, but she didn't look forward to meeting with her deceased ex-boyfriend's mom. The only other time she'd met the woman was after the funeral, which was awkward. Emma would keep their meeting brief. Because if she was going to be successful in putting that nightmare part of her life behind her, she needed to break all ties with BG's family.

~ ~ ~

On the return drive to Coastal Breeze, Thomas didn't turn on his radio. His thoughts made the miles go by. He smiled as he replayed his sister's conversation when he'd driven her to Alabama earlier that day. He couldn't remember when he'd heard Avril so vibrant, as she'd chattered non-stop about her visit. She'd been delighted to see her brother's new town, and she'd raved about Emma.

At the thought of Emma, Thomas had a

warmth and peace. Since apologizing to her for his harsh comments, he was ready to move forward with their relationship, and he hoped she felt the same.

His only concern now was the fact that Avril shared her ex-boyfriend's eagerness to resume their relationship. Not a good idea, in his opinion.

The ringing phone snapped Thomas from his musings. Although he didn't like to talk on his phone while driving, he was on a stretch of road with minimal traffic and the weather was clear. He answered, surprised to hear his mother's voice. Surely nothing was wrong, since things seemed fine when he took his sister home.

"Is everything okay, Mom?" He tried to keep worry out of his tone.

"Yes, dear. I'm sorry to bother you. Are you still on the road?"

"Yes, but it's okay. What is it?" His mother must have an important reason to phone him since they'd seen each other less than two hours ago.

"I didn't want to mention this in front of your sister, but I'm so worried about Devin coming back in the picture. Thinking of how he dumped her after the accident...well, it still makes my blood boil. I know I shouldn't say that, but as a mother it's how I feel." She blew out a breath.

"Do you think he's sincere? Or maybe he just feels guilty after the way he ditched her." Thomas had to be careful and remain focused on his driving and not let his thoughts from the past consume him.

"I'm not sure. Anyway, I didn't want to say anything in front of Avril when you brought her home today, and right now she's out front visiting with several of her friends from church. They were concerned when she wasn't there this morning."

A warm feeling ran through him at his mother's words, because he was grateful for his sister's church friends and their loyalty to her after the accident. In fact, they made sure she was included in various activities although she was limited to a wheelchair.

"I'm happy to hear her friends are visiting. Listen Mom, try not to worry too much about Devin. If necessary, I'll come home again soon and have a talk with him. There's no way I'm letting him build up my sister's hopes only to dump her again in the future."

His comments seemed to soothe his mother, and their call ended a few minutes later. He was relieved his mother hadn't mentioned Emma, because he was certain Avril would've mentioned her to his mom. Not that he was keeping his friendship with Emma a secret, but he didn't want his mother jumping to conclusions.

Yet at the back of his mind, Thomas imagined his mother and Emma being introduced, and was sure they'd hit it off, as his sister and Emma had the previous day. Now, if he'd watch his mouth and not blurt out any more hurtful comments to her, maybe their relationship could grow into something lasting. That thought made him smile as he continued his drive to Coastal Breeze.

~ ~ ~

"She's coming here? To Coastal Breeze?" Emma's voice rose an octave as she let Molly's news sink in her brain. Her best friend had phoned the following day informing Emma that BG's mother had decided to visit the Florida panhandle and would stop and see her. What was going on?

"I really hated to have to tell you this, but she's determined. When she stopped by my office today to tell me, I almost fell out of my chair. Whatever she wants to discuss with you is super important—at least to her. Poor woman...I can't help but feel sorry for her. She lost her son, and from everything we've heard, she hasn't had an easy life. Her eyes were misty as she spoke with me, all emotional. I'm sorry about this."

"It's not your fault. I guess I'll have to be prepared for her to show up at the gift shop, huh?"

"Yeah, sorry. But maybe whatever she needs to tell you will be brief and she'll be on her way."

After getting off the phone, Emma stared at her hands. How could she put her past completely behind her when her deceased ex-boyfriend's mother was coming to see her? *Pray.* The one-word silent reminder jolted her, and she felt a niggle of guilt. Yes, she needed to pray about whatever was going on with BG's mother, because as Molly had commented, the poor woman hadn't had an easy life. Emma would pray for the right words to say and a kind spirit while the woman talked. But she'd sure be relieved when this was over.

A sense of dread overwhelmed Emma on Friday, and she knew she wasn't trusting as she should. After all, she'd been praying about the expected visit from BG's mom ever since Molly had phoned her. It was possible that something might come up with her and she might not even visit.

Because the shop was fairly busy that day, Emma didn't have time to be still and allow her thoughts to roam. When she did have a few minutes to catch her breath, she tried to think about her upcoming date with Thomas that weekend. He'd mentioned they could drive over to another small community on the panhandle coast so she could snap some photos. The prospect of doing that thrilled her—mostly because she looked forward to spending more time with him.

It was late in the afternoon when the gift shop door opened and a tired-looking woman wearing jeans and a tee shirt entered. Her eyes darted around the shop before spotting Emma, who'd seen her at the same time.

Emma's pulse raced, and her mind whirled with thoughts. *Why did BG's mother want to see her? Would she stay very long?* Forcing a polite smile on her face, Emma walked toward the woman. "Hello, Ms. Grindle. May I help you with something?" How awkward she felt at that moment. A silent prayer rushed up as she tried to keep her hands and voice steady. *Lord, please help me say the right thing to this poor woman.*

Wendy Grindle reached up and pushed wayward strands of hair from her face. She offered a timid smile as she approached Emma. "Hi, Emma. I'm glad you're here. I'll only take a few minutes of your time. Is there some place we can sit?" She glanced around, obviously feeling out of place.

Just then, Aunt Ginny approached with a

cheery smile and welcomed the guest. She must have overheard the woman's question because Ginny nodded toward the supply room.

Emma led the way and the two women sat at a small table in one corner of the room. "May I get you something to drink? We have some bottled water in the fridge, and there should be soft drinks too." Even though she didn't want to prolong the woman's visit, she did want to be polite. Yet, relief washed over her when Ms. Grindle shook her head and mumbled "no thanks."

With a raspy voice from countless cigarettes, Wendy looked Emma in the eye and stammered, "I-I wanted to say thank you for all you did trying to help BG. He seemed to draw trouble to him, but I think you were a positive influence on him. Unfortunately, he inherited his weakness for drugs from his father, so he wasn't strong enough to stay away from that. But I know you were nice to him." Wendy hesitated a moment before continuing. "As you know, BG ran around with a bad group. That Mick and his gang were terrible for BG, and I'm glad those punks are all behind bars now, so you don't have to worry about seeing any of them." She paused as her eyes filled with unshed tears. "Anyway, I'm moving up to Kentucky to be with my relatives, so before I left Georgia, I wanted to find you, so I could say this to your face. You were the best thing that ever happened to BG. God bless you." She bolted to her feet and slid her chair underneath the table.

Emma's eyes filled with tears and she fought them as best she could. Slowly she stood too, not sure what to say to this pitiful woman who was trying to do the right thing.

Stepping around the table, Emma reached her arms around Wendy's shaking shoulders and hugged her, and Wendy didn't resist.

"I'm so sorry about what happened to BG, but I appreciate your visit today to share this with me. I hope you'll be very happy in Kentucky, and I'll pray for you."

With a weak chuckle, Wendy replied. "Thanks, Emma. I can sure use those prayers." Emma knew some of the smell from cigarettes would cling to her own clothes, but at the moment, it didn't matter. Poor Wendy needed that hug more than her clothes needed a wash.

Before exiting the supply room, Emma dashed over to the fridge and opened it, pleased to see a few soft drinks beside the bottled water. She grabbed two of each and grinned at Wendy. "I'll put these in a bag for you to take in your car. Your throat might get dry on the trip."

"Thank you. You're an angel. I do get thirsty when I'm driving." She hesitated as if unsure whether to say more, then shrugged. "And I'm trying to cut back on my cigarettes, so having something cold to drink will help with that too." She offered a weak smile.

After grabbing a bag to place the drinks in, Emma accompanied Ms. Grindle to the door. "Remember I'll be praying for you." She fought tears that were threatening to build again.

Wendy nodded her thanks. "I'm going to Georgia for a few days to finish packing, then will head on up to Kentucky." As she stepped out of the gift shop, she hesitated and looked back. "Thanks again, Emma. I sure hope you have a good life. You deserve it." Then she trudged to an older-model car that was in need of a coat of paint.

Emma was about to step inside the shop, when she paused. Standing over to her left, about fifteen feet away, was Thomas. He smiled, but a groove formed between his brows.

PATTI JO MOORE

9

Thomas wasn't sure what was going on, but he hoped Emma would share with him. But, as curious as he was, he wouldn't pry, although the woman who'd left the gift shop was not at all like the usual clientele. Maybe she was lost and had stopped to ask directions—that must be the reason Emma spoke with her and walked her to the door. No doubt about it—Emma Hopkins was the kindest person he'd ever met.

He stood out of the way while Emma rang up a sale for a customer who'd been waiting at the counter. Since he was next to a shelf with figurines, he picked up a few for a closer look, thinking Avril might enjoy the small dolphin. He replaced the figurines on the shelf, and returned his gaze to Emma.

Thomas observed her movements as she interacted with a middle-aged customer. Emma's smile came easily, showing a genuine compassion for others. She looked in his direction as he watched her, and embarrassment flooded him. After a quick smile, he forced his eyes away.

The customer left and Emma stepped around the counter to greet him. "This is a surprise. Did you have a nice day working?" Her sweet expression filled him with a warm joy.

"Yes, thanks. I had two appointments with clients and they both went well. I thought I'd stop by and make sure we're still on for dinner tomorrow. And I wanted to see where you'd like to eat." He still wondered if she'd share information about the tired-looking woman who'd left the gift shop a few minutes earlier.

"Sure, tomorrow for dinner sounds great. And I promise it doesn't matter where we eat—you can decide. Just let me know what time to be ready."

"How about six o'clock, and we can head to The Happy Fisherman?"

"Sounds great! I'll be ready." She must have needed to finish up some tasks before the shop closed because she eased back toward the counter. Thomas got the message. He said a quick good-bye and left.

Okay, no information about the mystery woman, but maybe at dinner the next day she'd reveal something. He wouldn't be so curious if not for the fact of the woman's appearance. She'd seemed haggard and pitiful—not at all the typical customer in the gift shop.

As soon as he arrived inside his bungalow, his cell phone rang. His mother's upbeat voice came through. "Hi Mom, is everything okay?" He felt certain it was from her tone.

"Oh yes. I hope I'm not interrupting anything, dear."

"No, this is perfect timing. I just came in the door so I wasn't in the middle of anything."

"Okay, good. I wanted to call and share something with you. I'd much prefer to tell you this in person, but I just can't wait. It's something I know you'll be very interested in learning." After a moment to catch her breath, Mrs. Wilton continued. "Devin came to visit us this afternoon. He'd asked ahead of time if it would be okay for him to speak with Avril and me, so I told him it was fine. He confessed that it was his text that your sister had been replying to when she had the horrible accident. He's carried the burden of guilt, and that's why he withdrew from her. Oh, you should've seen him. He had tears as he spoke. He begged Avril's forgiveness, and then begged for my forgiveness as well. He went on to say that when you're home again, he wants to meet with you and apologize. He was so remorseful, and your sister and I both began to cry. It was very emotional, but I think it was...." Her voice trailed off as she sniffled. "It was cleansing. I think that's the word I'm searching for. Devin needed to get that off his chest, and now we know what really happened. And you can release the guilt you've been carrying, dear. I know how this has eaten at you since Avril's accident, but there's no need for you to feel guilty any longer." More sniffles followed as his mother remained silent, waiting for him to reply.

It was a blessing he'd collapsed onto the sofa because his knees were weak, and tears blurred his vision. What his mother had shared was powerful. After carrying a load of guilt on his shoulders for the past three years, he could finally let it go. No, it didn't change his sister's situation. She was still in a wheelchair and bore the scars of the horrible accident. But Thomas no longer had to see her and think that he was the cause of her handicapped body.

"Son, are you there?" His mother's tone had changed to worry, and he realized she was awaiting his response.

"Yes, Mom. I'm sorry I didn't say anything yet—this is all sinking in. So you think Devin is sincere?" He didn't want to cast doubts, but had to make certain.

"I have no doubt at all. If you could've seen Devin as he opened up to us, you'd know for sure too. And Avril is accepting it quite well, especially considering what she's been through. After Devin left our house, your sister told me that she felt so sorry for him carrying that load of guilt. Now that he's admitted why he stayed away from her, she's open to seeing him again. And not only that, but Devin told us that he is more than willing to do whatever he can to help Avril get stronger. He has a relative who works in physical therapy, and she's going to visit Avril and offer some suggestions."

"Wow. This is all amazing, Mom. It does sound like Devin is sincere, and that's good that he came and talked with both of you. I still want Avril to be careful though. I don't want Devin or anyone else breaking her heart." His usual protectiveness would always remain for his sister.

"I know, dear. I feel the same way. And just between us, it thrills Avril that her big brother is so protective of her, even though she'd never say it to your face." His mother chuckled, and Thomas realized he was grinning.

After a few more minutes of chatting, the call ended. He remained seated on the sofa for a few more minutes, allowing this amazing revelation to sink in. *I am not the cause of my sister's accident. It's not my fault she's in a wheelchair.* The thoughts played over and over in his tired mind, and before leaving the sofa to fix a sandwich for his supper, Thomas offered up a prayer of thanks for the truth being revealed. He also prayed for Avril—that she would get even stronger and possibly walk one day.

Another thought struck Thomas as he ate his ham sandwich. A thought that filled him with joy. Now that he could release his burden of guilt, he could focus more on his relationship with Emma and not feel there was a cloud hanging over him. He was more at peace than he had been in a long, long time. And it was wonderful.

~ ~ ~

"What a gorgeous day!" Ginny glanced out the gift shop window the next morning and smiled. "I love this early June weather before the stifling heat takes over." She flipped the sign to OPEN and unlocked the door.

Emma grinned and nodded. She enjoyed the pretty weather too, and today was feeling rather lighthearted. After meeting with BG's mother the day before, she was relieved that was behind her and she was looking forward to having dinner at a restaurant that evening with Thomas. Yes, it was a very good day.

Later that afternoon, Emma went to the small refrigerator in the supply room to take a few sips of her bottled water. As she swallowed the cold liquid, she heard her cell phone buzz, indicating a text message. Hurrying to her handbag, she took out the phone and read the message from Molly, and then froze. Her friend's text informed her that Mick had escaped from prison, and the rumor was that he wanted to talk with BG's girlfriend. Unless her deceased ex-boyfriend had dated someone after her, that meant the escaped convict wanted to see her. Yet there was no reason for Mick to talk with her—she knew nothing.

Frantically punching in Molly's cell number, Emma knew her pulse was racing. She also needed to return to the gift shop area to help Ginny with customers.

"Emma? I'm so sorry I had to send that text to you. Are you okay?" Molly's voice held trepidation that only made Emma more nervous.

"Yes, I'm fine. But do you know any other details? I can't believe Mick escaped. Do you think he's really coming here? He has no reason to see me." She willed herself to stay as composed as possible. Giving in to tears would serve no purpose.

"Oh Emma…I hated putting that in my message, but that's what I heard. I just want you to be safe. Please be careful and let your aunt know. Let the police know too. They need to keep an eye on you—to keep you safe."

"Okay, I will. But I'd better go now because I'm supposed to be out in the gift shop area helping with customers. Thanks, Molly. Love you."

"Love you too, Em. Stay safe, girlfriend."

Shoving her phone back into her handbag, Emma hurried out to the shop to get back to work. Aunt Ginny eyed her curiously, and as soon as she finished speaking with a customer, rushed over to her niece.

"Emma Jean, are you okay? You look pale. Are you feeling sick?"

"Yes, I'll be okay. I'll explain when the shop closes."

At that moment, two women approached Ginny so she was unable to ask more questions, which was a relief. Emma had to collect her thoughts and decide what to do.

As soon as the last customer exited the shop, Ginny flipped the sign around to CLOSED and hurried to her niece. "Now, please tell me what's going on."

Emma did her best to explain Molly's phone message without sounding fearful.

"I am notifying our local police immediately, Emma Jean. They can at least keep an eye on you." Even as she spoke, Ginny cast a glance out the windows of the gift shop, as if making sure there wasn't an escaped convict lurking in the area.

"Okay. But I'll be fine, so I don't want you to worry. I've got a dinner date this evening with Thomas, and I'm certain when he brings me home, he'll make sure I get safely inside my cottage.

Besides, there's no reason for Mick to want to see me. I wasn't involved in any way with BG's dealings." Emma shook her head, knowing that she'd not convinced her aunt to refrain from worrying.

A short time later, both women left the gift shop and hurried to their cars. The bright June sunshine helped to keep thoughts of evil escapees at bay, and Emma forced herself to stay focused on her date in less than an hour. She'd freshen up her make-up, change clothes and shoes, and be ready when Thomas arrived. Just the thought of spending time with him this evening was a boost to her spirits.

Emma looked at her bedside clock. Thomas should be arriving within the next ten minutes, so she glanced one more time in the mirror to make sure her hair was smooth and she was wearing the right shade of lipstick. A knock at the front door sent her heart racing, and she couldn't help smiling at the thought of seeing her handsome businessman.

Pulling open her front door, Emma froze. The man standing on her doorstep was not Thomas, but rather a heavyset, gruff-looking man with tattoos on every visible area of his body, and a scowl on his face. Before Emma could react by slamming the door and locking it, the man shoved his way inside her cottage.

"I wanted to talk to you. I need some information and I need you to give it to me." A sneer followed his words and Emma's heart raced. She knew this had to be Mick, the escaped prisoner Molly had warned her about, and fear gripped her with icy fingers. There was no doubt she'd never been this scared in her life.

"I-I don't have any information." As the weak sentence flew out of her lips, she knew instantly her statement had only served to anger the thug now gripping her wrist.

"Oh, I think you do. BG hid some drug money, and you must know where it is. That money belongs to me, and I want it." His rough-skinned face was mere inches from Emma's and he reeked of strong alcohol. She had the urge to hold her breath, yet if she passed out, no telling what the crazed man might do then.

She didn't respond, but silently prayed more earnestly than she ever had. *Please, Lord. Please keep me safe.* From the way this man looked and spoke, she knew that trying to reason with him would be pointless.

His eyes bulged, and he tightened his grip. "Look, I went to a lot of trouble to find you, so I want answers. Where is that money? It belongs to me." He emitted a low growl and shook her, then cursed.

An endless moment of tension hung in the air. What should she do? What could she do except keep praying? Surely her pounding heart would explode any second.

Then, her front door burst open. Thomas, along with three policemen, rushed in. In the blink of an eye, Mick released Emma and took off running out her door and toward the street. Thomas grabbed Emma and held her close to him, gently patting her back. Two of the police chased after Mick. The third checked the rest of the cottage to make certain no one else was hiding.

"Freeze and raise your hands!" One of the police yelled to Mick. A gunshot rang out, followed by another gunshot. Emma cringed, and her legs gave out. Sobs wracked through her body. Would this nightmare ever end? Would she ever be able to put the past behind her?

~ ~ ~

"Here, have another shrimp and you'll feel better." Thomas reached across the small table in Emma's cottage and fed her a shrimp. His gaze lingered on her face, and she read love in his eyes.

After she swallowed, Emma giggled. "Oh? Is that some kind of proven theory? That after a person endures a horrific ordeal, they'll feel better if they eat shrimp?" She couldn't resist teasing him. Since the terrible incident three hours earlier, Thomas had doted on her as she'd never been doted on in her life. And it felt wonderful, despite her exhaustion.

He gave her a playful wink and nodded. "Yes, I think so. Now, you let me know when you're ready for a slice of lemon pie, okay?" He gently squeezed her shoulder, and Emma knew he wanted to make sure she was indeed okay.

When Mick had fired a shot at the police, one of them had no choice but to fire in self-defense, and the escaped prisoner had been killed. Tragic, but something that would not have happened if Mick would've complied.

Hours passed as the police taped the crime scene, questioned Emma and filed reports, and the medical examiner was brought in. Now only Thomas remained at her cottage. She'd declined his offer to go out to eat, so Aunt Ginny had contacted several church members who'd kindly driven to The Happy Fisherman and picked up meals to-go, delivering them to Emma's door. Her aunt had stayed until Emma insisted she'd be fine. But Thomas wouldn't leave her side and offered to sleep in his car parked in her driveway if necessary.

A little before midnight, Emma assured Thomas she'd be fine, and hopefully would be able to sleep. He made her promise to keep the phone beside her and call him if she felt uneasy. Once her head was on the pillow, it wasn't long before she fell into a deep slumber, awaking the next morning to her ringing phone.

"I'm so sorry if I woke you, but I had to make sure you're okay." Thomas's voice held concern.

Suppressing a yawn, she replied. "I'm fine, I promise. Are we still on for taking that ride today?"

"You bet! I'll drive you anywhere you'd like to go." The joy in his voice was obvious, causing her to smile as she held the phone.

After he came by, they picked up doughnuts and coffee for breakfast, then spent the day riding along the panhandle coast, stopping at various spots for Emma to snap photographs. An early supper at a seafood restaurant in Destin completed the picture-perfect day before returning to Coastal Breeze.

Pulling into Emma's driveway, Thomas cast a sheepish glance at her. "Are you too tired for a quick walk on the beach? I figure we've got some good daylight left, and there's nothing like a sunset over the gulf."

She couldn't hold back a laugh. "You sound like a person who's been living here at the coast for quite a while, rather than a newcomer." Then she added. "And yes, a walk on the beach will be lovely."

As they headed to the usual path that led to the sandy shore, Thomas gently took her hand in his. "Your comment a few minutes ago made me think. I know I haven't lived here long, but I've already decided that I've fallen in love with this area. I really think I want to continue living here—maybe forever." He paused and smiled down at Emma. They'd reached the beach area and inched toward the water's edge.

"Oh really? That's nice to hear. I really enjoy living here too." With a racing heart, she attempted to keep her voice casual, yet she wasn't sure where his conversation was headed because he was acting a bit mysterious.

He stopped and turned to face her. Water lapped at their feet and the seagulls soared overhead. Thomas cleared his throat and gazed directly into her eyes. "You know something else I've fallen in love with? You." He leaned down and kissed her, slowly and tenderly, then gently pulled back and smiled.

Emma thought she might melt onto the sand. *He loved her!* And she knew there was no denying it—she loved him too.

With tears of joy filling her eyes, Emma gazed up into the face of the man she had not known a long time, but the one who held her heart. "I love you too, Thomas."

He took her hand again and led her a few steps forward. There was only the sound of the waves and seagulls around them as the sunset graced the western sky. Thomas stopped and faced her again before bowing onto one knee. "Emma Hopkins, will you marry me? I've known for a while that I loved you, but when I saw you in danger last night, I knew, without a doubt, that I want to spend the rest of my life protecting you, being with you, and giving you all my love."

Tears streamed down Emma's face as she beamed and nodded. "Yes! I'll marry you, Thomas Wilton." Now, in addition to the waves rolling in and the seagulls overhead, there was applause. Unbeknownst to the couple, a small group of beachgoers had gathered not far away and were observing them. Now the group clapped and offered their congratulations.

Emma was happier than she'd ever been in her life, and was thankful that the Lord had led her and Thomas both to this small coastal town—to give them a seaside romance to last forever.

EPILOGUE

"Oh Emma, you look beautiful. And now I'll finally have a sister!" Avril beamed at the bride standing beside her.

"I'm glad we'll be sisters too, Avril. And you're a beautiful maid of honor." Emma leaned over and gave a quick hug to Thomas's sister, looking lovely in her teal bridesmaid gown and standing with the use of a cane. Then Emma added in a whisper. "I wouldn't be surprised if you're wearing a wedding gown before long." She almost giggled as Avril ducked her head and blushed, then realized Devin was observing them with a grin.

Molly hurried over to the women, her bridesmaid gown not able to conceal the fact she was five months pregnant. "You picked the perfect time for a wedding, girlfriend. October is just right—not hot, but not too chilly." She grinned at her best friend, then turned her attention to Avril.

"You're getting a wonderful sister-in-law, and I'm sure Emma thinks the same about you." The three women chuckled before Devin joined them.

"Hate to break up this little party, but the minister said the ceremony is about to begin, so you'd better head for the door. I'm taking a seat with the guests." His eyes lingered on Avril before he leaned over and placed a quick peck on her cheek.

As her father took her arm to walk her down the aisle, Emma thought she surely must be dreaming. Not only was she marrying a handsome man she loved with all her heart, but she already loved his family too. The fact that Avril was no longer confined to a wheelchair all the time was a miracle in itself, thanks in large part to Devin's devoted help in obtaining excellent physical therapy for her. And to try and bring good from a serious situation, the couple had agreed to visit local schools and talk to the students about the dangers of texting while driving.

Before heading down the aisle, Emma caught sight of dear Aunt Ginny, dabbing her nose with a linen handkerchief and seated beside Mr. Grover. A budding romance for certain, Emma thought with a smile. She knew Ginny was thrilled that the newlyweds would continue residing in Coastal Breeze, and Emma could keep her job at the gift shop.

As the bride joined her groom at the altar of the Coastal Breeze church, the couple only had eyes for each other. When the brief but sweet ceremony was over, everyone gathered in the church fellowship hall for a reception.

Midge was one of the first guests to congratulate the newly-married couple. "Oh my, who would think that two people could meet and fall in love in a small community, such as Coastal Breeze? How wonderful and amazing at the same time, considering our population isn't even two thousand." She cackled and grinned at the couple.

As soon as the older woman walked away, Thomas leaned over to his bride. "I have a feeling, Mrs. Wilton, that in the coming years, the Coastal Breeze population might very well increase, thanks to today's wedding." He winked at her as she blushed. But she had to agree, because having a family with Thomas would make their seaside romance complete.

THE END

PATTI JO MOORE

After teaching the first grade and kindergarten for 21 years, Patti Jo had to retire early due to severe spinal problems. She saw this as an opportunity to fulfill her dream of writing full-time, which she loves. A life-long Georgia girl, Patti Jo loves Jesus, her family, and cats. The Lord blessed her abundantly this year with her very first grandbaby and her first writing contract. She's excited about being a Forget-Me-Not Author, and is looking forward to connecting with lots of readers. This is her first novel.

www.ingramcontent.com/pod-product-compliance
Lightning Source LLC
LaVergne TN
LVHW012018060526
838201LV00061B/4359